# HERE IT ENDS

## A NOVEL BY DAN LAWTON

Black Rose Writing | Texas

ISBN: 978-1-68513-202-6
PUBLISHED BY BLACK ROSE WRITING
www.blackrosewriting.com

Printed in the United States of America
Suggested Retail Price (SRP) $20.95

*Here It Ends* is printed in Plantagenet Cherokee

*As a planet-friendly publisher, Black Rose Writing does its best to eliminate unnecessary waste to reduce paper usage and energy costs, while never compromising the reading experience. As a result, the final word count vs. page count may not meet common expectations.

THAT WAS BEFORE

A NOVEL BY DAN LAWTON

*For Dad*

# HERE IT ENDS

HERE IT ENDS

# CHAPTER ONE

*Fifteen years ago.* An eleven-year-old girl stood in her mother's kitchen while her father packed her backpack. She felt the tug against her shoulders as he filled the secret compartment at the bottom. Inside the secret compartment was a smaller compartment accessible with a unique three-digit code. The code was unique each time. She knew her father had the master code that would open the compartment every time, overriding the temporary one. He changed the temporary code every time he filled up her backpack. It was for her safety, he said once.

A teapot whistled on the stovetop. Her mother finished what she was doing and scampered toward it with a teacup in hand. The steam billowed against the ceiling when boiling water cascaded over the bag in her mother's cup. It smelled like the garden. Her father spoke something in Finnish to her mother, but the girl did not understand what it meant. Her parents spoke Finnish only when there was a conversation they did not want their only child to be a part of. Otherwise, they spoke English. Everyone the girl knew spoke English, including everyone at her school.

Being an only child, the girl often felt lonely at home. Her father was frequently on the phone in his office on the other side of the house, and her mother kept busy being a homemaker. After school, the girl would sit at the dinner table in the kitchen and work on her studies while her mother prepared dinner—or as her mother called it, middag. On days her father packed her backpack, he would be waiting for her on the front stoop when she arrived home. She would walk to and from most days, except for the ones her mother deemed too cold. Or the rainy ones. On those days, her mother would drive her. Those days were the girl's favorites. She enjoyed the extra time with her mother, even if it was often without conversation.

On this day, the girl felt a twinge of excitement as she stood in the kitchen. The smaller secret compartment clicked at her back. The buttons popped on the larger one. Her father kissed her on the head and left the kitchen without saying anything to her. Now that she had a year under her belt at the comprehensive school and knew what to expect, the nerves she felt on this day the year before were gone. She had heard nothing but good things about the teacher she would be having this year. Plus, her best friend was going to be in class with her, so that made her happy. She had not seen her, or any of her friends, all summer long.

Her mother put her teacup down and made a twirling motion with her finger. The girl spun around and faced the hallway. She sensed her mother approach from the back. The tug on her shoulders was stronger, the backpack heavier, as her mother loaded the pack with the school supplies she needed for the year. After she was zipped, the girl spun and faced her mother, who smiled at her.

"Have a wonderful first day, sweetheart," her mother said.

The girl smiled at her.

"I'll make ostkaka for dessert to celebrate."

"With blueberries?"

Her mother smiled again. She knew it was the girl's favorite. "Of course. Now go on. You don't want to be late."

"Yes, Mother." The girl turned back toward the hallway and began to walk. As she approached the front door, her father popped his head out from his office.

"Sheila?" he said.

She stopped.

He handed her a slip of scrap paper with three digits on it— the temporary code for the secret compartment in her backpack. She took it and slid it into her sock. Even if her skirt had pockets, the sock was safer; no one would look there.

"There will be someone to meet you at the barber shop after school. You know it?"

"Yes, Daddy."

Her father smiled. "That's my good girl."

The girl waited for her father to retreat to his office. Once he did, she reached for the door handle, twisted it, and stepped outside.

She was ready for her first day of fifth grade.

•    •    •    •    •

School came and went. Sheila was pleased to see her best friend and was impressed how much she had grown up—and it seemed the boys were too. At lunch, she heard a group of them whispering about the small bumps on her chest that protruded through her shirt. Sheila did not know what it meant but noticed her friend seemed embarrassed all day; she did not unzip her coat once. Sheila's chest still looked like the boys'.

The teacher was nice, but they all were on the first day. One of the boys farted in class and made the other boys laugh. None of the girls thought it was as funny as the boys, including the teacher. The boy was scolded in front of everyone and forced to excuse himself in front of the entire class. For the rest of the day, he slouched at his desk and kept his head down. Sheila did not know the boy, but she felt bad for him. If it were her in that situation, she would have felt terribly embarrassed.

After the dismissal bell rang, Sheila left school and walked to the barber shop. Most kids would have been afraid to go the barber shop without an adult, but not Sheila. This was not her first time, and she was sure it would not be the last. The locations rotated—if not the barber shop, it could be the country store or the supermarket, or a gas station. On the rare occasion, Sheila would be given change and instructed to take public transportation to a certain location somewhere in town. After the transfer was made, she would ride to a different location, where her mother or father would meet her with the car. On those days, her mother would often pack her an extra snack for the ride, in case she got hungry.

A trio of men smoked cigarettes outside the barber shop. Only one of them looked at her. Black teeth popped out from behind his lips.

"I'm looking for Astrid," Sheila said.

The man with the blackened teeth laughed. "You? How do you know Astrid?"

"Is he here or not?"

The other two smoky men looked at her now. One of them blew a gray cloud out from his nostrils. The other gave a curt smile.

"Come on," the man with the blackened teeth said.

She followed him inside the barber shop without a second thought. The truth was, Sheila had no reason to be afraid. If the men her father sent her to see wanted whatever it was her father wanted them to have, then they would do as her father asked. Only once had someone tried to get handsy with her. That was a few months before, shortly after she began helping out her father; not long after her eleventh birthday. He grabbed her by the waist and had a look in his eye that frightened her.

Thankfully, another man was there and pushed him off her and shouted at him in Finnish. The handsy man dropped his head and apologized in English to Sheila, who did not accept his apology but completed the transfer anyhow.

When she arrived home, her father must have seen something in her expression that caused alarm, because his eyes grew wide and he ran to the car and sped out of the driveway. An hour later, he came back home and insisted Sheila go to her room. Sheila listened through the grate in the floor and heard her parents frantically speaking in Finnish. The faucet ran on full blast in the kitchen and Sheila thought she heard her mother scrubbing. Not long after, footsteps climbed the stairs and Sheila hurried onto her bed and pretended to brush a doll's hair. The bathroom door opened and closed, and the shower turned on. She heard the pipes click through the wall as they always did when the hot water ran through them. Later, before bed, her father told her that nothing like what happened to her the day before would ever happen again. He promised, even though he did not ask what happened or if she was all right. But she believed him.

So far, her father was right. Which was why she was not afraid to follow the man with the bad teeth into the back room of the barber shop. Sheila kept her eyes straight ahead, purposefully not observing her surroundings; as her father frequently told her, the less she knew, the better.

"Astrid, you have a visitor," the man said.

A large man taller than her father appeared from around the filing cabinet. He took one look at Sheila, then at the man who escorted her in. "Don't smoke that shit in here."

The man with the disgusting teeth removed the cigarette from his mouth and cupped it in his hand. "Sorry."

"Now go."

The man turned around and quickly left, leaving a smoky trail in his wake.

"Sorry about him," the man Sheila assumed to be Astrid said. "And for my language before. I shouldn't have said 'shit.'"

Sheila did not know what to say, so she said nothing.

"Do you have something for me?"

"Yes."

Astrid folded his arms. His muscles bulged. Sheila bent down and reached into her sock. She pinched the scrap paper between two fingers and pulled it out, then handed it to Astrid. She slid her backpack off her shoulders and dropped it on the desk in front of her. She unzipped the back and withdrew her school supplies, neatly stacking them on the desk. When she got to the bottom where the secret compartments were, she unsnapped the buttons on the outside one and slid the material to the side so the dial for the code was visible. Then she turned the pack toward Astrid and stepped back.

He reached inside and fumbled around, his eyes darting between the scrap of paper in his hand and the bottom of the backpack. Eventually, the compartment clicked. Astrid's eyes lit up. Sheila slid the straps over her shoulders and turned her back as she was instructed to do while Astrid did whatever he had to do. She felt the weight of her backpack steadily increase and yanked on the straps to help ease the discomfort on her lower back. A familiar click sounded again. Buttons snapped. That was her cue.

She slid the backpack off again and faced Astrid briefly, then tossed the pack back on the desk. She refilled it with her school supplies and zipped it.

"Goodbye, now," Astrid said.

"Goodbye."

Sheila left the barber shop and walked home.

• • •

Her father greeted her on the stoop. He gently draped his arm around her shoulder and led her into the house. From there, she followed the routine without needing to be told. She gave her backpack to her father, who took it and retreated into his office and closed the door; she kicked off her shoes and put them in the basket near the door; she went into the bathroom and washed her hands and face; then she went into the kitchen and greeted her mother with a kiss on the cheek. When her father was ready, he would return the backpack—much lighter—and she would work on her studies.

The day after that was the same, as was the day after that. Some weeks, she would have somewhere to be after school every day. Other weeks, it would only be once or twice. Each night, her mother spooned her a thick, sticky medicine before bed that would help her from falling ill. Sheila had never missed a day of school for as long as she could remember. Even on days she felt sick, if her father gave her a scrap of paper in the morning, it was Sheila's responsibility to fight through it.

"We all have a responsibility to this family," her father said once. "This is yours. Do you understand?"

"Yes, Daddy."

"That's my good girl."

It went on like that every day. Until two years later, when Sheila turned thirteen. She arrived home from school and met her parents in the kitchen. They had something to tell her, her mother said. Then nothing was the same after that.

# CHAPTER TWO

*Present day.* There was blue as far as the eye could see, on all sides. It had been nearly two straight weeks of it. Randolph had never felt claustrophobic before now, but two weeks at sea had that effect on him. Despite 1,000 feet of endless entertainment and all the food he could eat and drinks at every corner—though he stuck to water in recent days, mostly—and open sky, he felt suffocated. Trapped. Whether it was the thousands of people on board or the constant noise or the sensation of always being in motion, he was ready to put his feet back on solid ground.

The cruise ship docked every so often at ports that all looked the same, felt the same, and smelled the same. Tens of hundreds of passengers lined up with their fanny packs strapped around their waists, transparent sarongs covering their bikinis, lovers by their side. Some people laughed and pressed their lips against their partner's. Others held hands. Many flirted. Love and happiness were everywhere around him.

He did not feel the same way.

It was not that he had the expectation that he and Sheila would rekindle their lust from their road trip across the Midwest, because he had no expectations at all. He was there out of fear—

fear that Gary O'Reilly was up to no good, that he was out to sabotage Randolph in some way. As Sheila explained to him in Utah, Gary was who he said he was in that he did work for INTERPOL, but it was what he did outside of his work for INTERPOL that was the problem. Gary had a history of recruiting people from all levels of authority to help him—investigators, police officers, private citizens—get what he wanted, then discarding them. Not just discarding them in the traditional sense; they disappeared.

And according to Sheila, Randolph was next.

Whether he believed everything she said was not exactly the point. What motivated him was one simple question: What if she was right? For that, he was not willing to risk it.

Spending two weeks together on the cruise ship hardly felt like it. There was not much togetherness. Sheila spent an unfathomable amount of time huddled up with a mobile phone or a laptop. He would find her in the corner of one of the restaurants, or by the pool, or sometimes just in the room, always by herself. Most often she would ignore him and continue what she was doing. Other times, she would look up and smile but not say anything.

On a ship with 3,000 other people, Randolph felt completely alone.

They would meet up for dinner most nights, or for a sporadic drink. The conversation would mostly flow around the happenings on the ship—the live shows that day or the celebrity sightings or the games or arguments that broke out on deck—or the big spenders at the casino. There was very little of significance about Gary or what they had been through or where they were going. He found the whole charade infuriating.

There was a decision to make. He knew they would be at their final destination within the next twenty-four hours. The agreement from the beginning was that if Randolph did not like what he heard, if he did not agree with the plan or understand the mission, he would go back home. When they got where they were going, back to land, Randolph could fly home to Iowa and call his lawyer and get this resolved through proper legal channels.

Or he could stay. He could trust Sheila knew what she was doing, and that what she said was the truth. He could trust the process. She would not have gone out of her way to warn him about Gary the way she did if there was not some truth to it—he reminded himself of that frequently, especially when the doubt creeped in. Their relationship was complicated, no doubt, and built on a foundation of deception. But that did not mean the emotions they shared had to be too. For as much as he doubted himself and his reasons for feeling the way he did, he trusted Sheila. Deep down, somewhere even he had a hard time identifying, he did. For all her dishonesties, they were all for protection—for herself, certainly, but also for his. Which was not something he could say for Gary.

So when it came down to it, it really was not much of a decision at all.

Across the room, the lock snapped. Randolph turned away from the window and toward the sound. In walked Sheila. Something was different about her—he noticed it immediately. She looked lighter, happier, more at ease. Before, she carried tension that weighed her down like an anchor, slumping her shoulders and tugging her downward. Now, that was gone, as if that weight had been lifted.

"Hi," she said. A smile creeped across her face.

"Hi."

"What are you doing?"

"Just sitting. Enjoying the view."

"We dock tomorrow."

"I know."

"Looking forward to it?"

"Very much."

"Me too."

Sheila loosely folded her arms, her fingers hugging her wrists. "So should—"

"Sheila, I—"

They both stopped. Waited.

"You go first," Randolph said.

"No, you go."

"Okay. Listen, I—"

"I know what you're going to say, and you're right."

"You do?"

"I've been distant. Really distant. And I have. But there's a reason. You have to trust me on that. I'm setting us up for the next leg of this. I have to admit, it's taken longer than I thought. I hit some snags along the away."

"Snags?"

"Nothing for you to worry about. It's all worked out now. Everything's all set."

"Sheila, I still don't even know where we're going or what we're doing or if I want to go. You said we were going to talk about everything, but we've talked hardly at all. I still don't know if I trust you or if—"

"Randolph."

He was on his feet now, pacing back and forth between the sofa and the small space that separated him and Sheila. "One minute I think you're right but the next I wonder what if you're not and then—"

"Randolph."

"I'm feeling suffocated in this tiny room with all these people and it's been burning a little when I pee but only sometimes not always and then I wonder if it's just because I'm dehydrated but probably not because all I've had for three days is water and—"

"Randolph!"

He stopped, caught his breath. What was he saying?

"Calm down. You're fine. We're fine. Everything's fine."

He looked at her. Then she did the thing, the thing that always made him stop and rebalance himself—she smiled at him. It was the same smile that began his infatuation in Iowa; the same smile that led him to travel across the country with her; the same smile that brought him to where he was, right now, with the blue of the ocean on either side of him that seemed as if it had no end.

"That's what I wanted to say to you," Sheila said. "I promised we'd talk and that I'd tell you everything you wanted to know. And I meant it."

"We're docking tomorrow."

"Right. Which means we still have tonight. I thought we could grab a good dinner, maybe a bottle of wine, and just talk. For as long as you want."

"Tonight?"

She smiled again. "Tonight."

He thought about it. It did not take long. "Okay. That sounds good." And it did. "Tonight then."

# CHAPTER THREE

*Present day.* It was a rental. A different rental. A better rental. Although if Benji was honest with himself, just about anything would have been better than his old raggedy apartment in the city. He was still in the city somewhere, downtown, five floors up and overlooking the river. It was the same building Gary O'Reilly brought him and Randolph to once upon a time not that long ago.

It felt like forever ago when he and Randolph sat in Gary's office in the inconspicuous building without signage and became partners. It was inside the same office where Randolph slugged Benji square in the jaw and drew blood. Their relationship could not have started off rockier. Benji smiled and laughed to himself at the memory. In retrospect, he deserved it. Just as quickly as the laughter came, a pang of sadness took over. While the beginning was rough, Benji felt there was a genuine, father-son-like relationship that had formed between them when they were in Fiji. Even when Randolph flaked out and took off without a trace once they were back in the States, Benji still had a soft spot for the man. It was not exactly guilt for Benji's role in the ultimate demise of Randolph's marriage, because in fairness, he did not know about it at the time. With Patricia—or Cheyenne, as he knew her to be then—it was all physical. Patricia was a sexual deviant. A freak. And he took advantage of that. Just like she too took advantage of that, and him—just differently.

Benji was a pawn in Patricia's sick game. A game that was supposed to end with Randolph, her then husband, dead. Benji's role in the con was more involved than he would have liked to acknowledge, but he could not escape the truth. It was he, ultimately, who built the mini pipe bomb and planted it inside the pen. It was he who designed the timer for the detonator. It was he who set it off. Thanks to Sheila's carelessness—Sheila, whom he knew as Shay at the time—Randolph did not take the pen with the explosive device with him. Because of that mistake, his truck did not explode with him inside, which would have in all likelihood killed him. Instead, the pen was left inside the supermarket. When it detonated, it set off a frenzy inside. But thankfully, since it was designed to be small enough to take out one man inside one truck, it was not large enough to cause any significant damage to the supermarket—or more importantly, anyone inside. Because of her mistake, Benji was not a killer. Unfortunately for him, the courts did not see intent and execution as much different.

As much as he tried to forget about it and move on with his life—chalk it up to a stupid decision by a stupid kid—doing so was all but impossible. Thanks to Gary, he was out of jail. For now. For whatever strings Gary pulled to get that done—Gary worked for INTERPOL, but not as a special agent because there was no such thing, he said; it was complicated—that now meant Benji was his hostage. First it was Fiji with Randolph to try to track down Sheila and help bring her to justice—whatever that meant to Gary. That mission failed. Sheila resurfaced in Colorado, but she slipped through their fingers again.

Now, Benji was back in Iowa where it all began, and sharing an office with the man who both got him out of jail but also owned him in every respect. If Benji did not agree to help him try to track down Sheila a second time, the threat of being sent back to jail and having the entire supermarket explosion and attempted murder of Randolph pinned on him hung over his head. Helping again also meant going after Randolph too, who disappeared in Colorado, seemingly either with Sheila's assistance or with her directly.

Either way, Benji was put in an impossible spot: sacrifice himself or sacrifice the man he grew to know and like and looked to as a mentor. But that was not the worst of it. Helping Gary O'Reilly again was one thing. Did Benji trust him? Not at all. He sensed Gary was into shady business and lived on the edge of the law by misusing whatever power he had, although he had no proof of that. What made this whole situation gut-wrenching was who his new partner was. It was Patricia—Randolph's now ex-wife, Benji's ex-lover; the mastermind behind the original plot to execute her husband for financial gain. It was truly the epitome of working for the enemy.

But Benji's life depended on his cooperation.

The memories twisted the knife of regret into his gut. He did not want to be there. He was set up with his computer and Gary could get him access to any government database he needed, or so he said. Add Benji's skills to the access he was promised to be granted, and it did not seem like finding Randolph would be difficult. That was their first objective—to find Randolph. Sheila had proven to be a true professional and could expertly stay off the grid. She had countless aliases and had been smart enough to stay if not one but two steps ahead of Gary and all his access thus far. Randolph, on the other hand, was a complete amateur. Which meant it was only a matter of time before he would make a mistake.

The working theory was that Randolph and Sheila were in cahoots. Gary had reached out to him and given him multiple opportunities to make contact and tell Gary what was going on, but all those attempts went unanswered—according to Gary. Randolph was avoiding him. It did not take a genius to connect the dots. Sheila popped up in Colorado, then Randolph disappeared without a trace just hours after contact with her was supposed to have been made. Benji did not want to believe it, but he was not blind, either. He hoped for a logical explanation; Randolph was, after all, one of the most logical people Benji had ever known.

When they found Randolph, he would surely have an explanation to have this all make sense—why he disappeared and fell off the grid. Benji wondered if he was in trouble. That was what he tried to convince himself of—that he was doing good, to find Randolph and help him. The other, more sinister side of him feared what Gary suspected—that finding Randolph would lead them directly to Sheila, one way or another. The sooner they found Randolph, the sooner they would find Sheila, and the sooner this would all finally be over. Gary could do whatever it was he needed to do with Sheila, then everyone could go their separate ways. Which meant Benji could go back to Fiji and reconnect with the girl of his dreams.

*Justice.*

This was what this was all about. Justice for Randolph for all he had been through; justice for Sheila for all she had put others through; and Justice for Benji, one person he could see himself loving. Gary would get what he so desperately wanted after having chased Sheila for years, but that was not a priority as far as Benji was concerned.

As for Patricia, he failed to see why she was there and how she added value. Patricia was not a good person. She was evil. It seemed Gary did her a solid by manufacturing evidence that could be used to raise doubt as to her guilt in the plot to have her husband killed. She told Gary that she was the person who knew Randolph the best in this world—which was hard to argue with—and that made her the best candidate to get him to talk. To talk about what? Benji wondered. She and Gary spun it as if Randolph had something to do with all of this, as if he coconspired with Sheila in some way. After having spent so much time together and working closely with him, Benji could not fathom that possibility. It was Randolph who pushed Benji to focus when they were in Fiji; it was Randolph who wanted to find Sheila the most; it was Randolph who had unfinished business with her, loose ends to tie up.

Benji was there from the beginning, and there was no way—no possible way—that Randolph was involved in any of it. He could not have been convinced of it, no matter the theories Gary and Patricia tried to concoct. Randolph was the one victim out of everyone involved. So while they were a team, Benji was working alone. He kept his doubts to himself and did what Gary asked him to do—which was staying glued to his computer and using all the resources he had to find Randolph. He tried not to concern himself with what Gary and Patricia were busying themselves with.

Benji sensed someone behind him. Fresh aftershave hit his nose first, the spice of it too strong for his liking. Then he felt the chair swivel ever so slightly. He turned and looked over his shoulder at Gary, who had a hand on the back of the chair. His button-down was uncharacteristically untucked from his pleated khakis, a corner dangling over his hip. His hair was disheveled and crusty, the hairspray not masking his lack of cleanliness. The bags under his eyes told Benji that Gary was exhausted.

"What's the latest?" Gary asked. His breath was minty-fresh.

"No change in status," Benji said. A map of the continental United States lit up his computer screen, but no red dots illuminated. A separate, smaller map that scrolled through the islands and territories was in the bottom corner of his second monitor. If Randolph or Sheila popped up anywhere in a United States territory, Benji would see it.

"Damn. Keep working."

Benji studied him. "You look awful. When was the last time you slept?"

"Don't worry about me."

"You should get yourself a coffee."

"I don't drink coffee."

"Maybe you should start."

Gary smirked. It looked like he might laugh, but he did not.

"What's Patricia doing?" Benji asked. "I mean, why is she even here?"

Gary no longer smirked. "I'll be the one asking the questions, Benjamin. Just do what you're told."

Benji held his hands up in surrender.

"Let me know right away if you get anything. Anything at all."

"You got it, boss."

"Don't call me boss."

"No problem, boss."

Gary's jaw flexed, but he did not retort. He turned his shoulders and walked away. Benji smiled and swiveled back toward the monitors. Sometimes, you had to make the best of a shitty situation. And with this shitty situation, busting Gary's balls as much as possible felt like an appropriate response.

# CHAPTER FOUR

*Thirteen years ago.* When Sheila arrived home that day when she was thirteen, she knew something was different. There was no drop-off that day, so she went right home after school. It was a sunny day, unseasonably warm. She remembered hurrying home, hoping her mother would let her do some reading on the porch in the back before the sun went down. If she promised to help clean the dishes after dinner and discuss her day with her mother then, she hoped her mother would agree. There were not many nice days left during that time of the year.

Sheila kicked off her shoes, slid out of her jacket, and called for her mother.

"In here, sweetheart," her mother called from the kitchen. The tone in her mother's voice was different. More chipper. Fuller of life. Usually, her mother was stoic, seldom layered with emotion. The change was noteworthy.

Sheila entered the kitchen. A pie was baking. There was a vase of her mother's favorite flowers on the counter—the cornflower. Its petals were as blue as the ocean, almost purple when the sunlight hit them just right through the window. At first, Sheila did not notice her parents sitting at the kitchen table, both of them, holding hands. Something was definitely up; Sheila hardly ever saw them show affection for one another.

"What's going on?" Sheila asked with concern.

Her mother smiled. "Sit down. Join us. Your daddy and me have some news."

Sheila felt her heart in her chest beat faster and harder than normal. Thump, thump, thump. She hoped her parents did not see her hands shaking as she walked around the table and pulled up a chair. The legs screeched as they slid across the floor.

"We received some exciting news today," her mother said, as if she had not already said it.

"What is it?"

Sheila's mother looked at her father with a smile Sheila had not seen in a while—one filled with love and happiness and admiration. Her father returned something similar. They were still holding hands. When her mother returned her gaze to her only child, tears filled them.

"We found out today," she said, "that we're going to have another baby."

The words hung in the air like a missile. That was not possible.

"I thought you said—"

"Yes, sweetheart, I thought so—we, thought so too. We didn't think we could have another baby after you."

Sheila did not know what to say. "I don't know what to say."

"It's lovely news, isn't it, sweetheart?"

"Well, yes . . . yes, it is good news."

"You're going to be a big sister," her father added.

Which was true. She had not thought much about that since her parents told her years before that she would be an only child—they were unable to have other children, they said. Had Sheila wanted a brother or sister to play with? She was not sure. She was thirteen now. She had made it that far by herself, on her own. As a girl, she daydreamed about having a sister to play dolls with, or a brother to play army men with during that short phase she had. But she never thought it would happen, so she had not thought about that in a long time.

*Big sister.*

The idea of it intrigued her. Would she be a good sister? How would she know how to hold the baby? Many questions scrambled through her mind, all at once. The library had books to help new parents, she knew, but did they have similar ones for new sisters? She could ask the nice librarian lady at school. Would it be a boy or a girl? Could it be twins? Triplets! What would her mother do? Where would the baby sleep? There were so many details to figure out.

"What do you think?" her father asked.

"I think . . . I think it's good news." She knew that was not what her parents wanted to hear, but she did not know what else to say. Was it good news? She was not sure yet. She needed some private time to think about it before she could decide.

She felt something touch her skin. She looked down and saw a hand on top of hers. Her father's.

"It's okay," her father said. "It's unexpected. We understand that. It's unexpected for us too. But another child, another member of our family, that's good news."

"Yes, Daddy." She was sure he was right. He was always right. Even if sometimes she did not think he was right.

He smiled at her and patted the top of her hand. "That's my good girl."

.   .   .   .   .

Later that evening, when she lay in her bed in the darkness, unable to sleep, she thought about the news from the afternoon. The more she thought about it, the more she thought her father was indeed right—it was good news. Part of her felt guilty for not believing him before, although she knew he was right. That had been happening more and more—her not believing he was right. She would never tell him that, though, because she was a good daughter and good daughters did not challenge the decisions their fathers made.

Her eyes adjusted to the darkness. She saw the outline of her dresser and the shelf with all her favorite knickknacks, and the smaller shelf with all her books. There was only one window in her room, and it was on the far side of the room, opposite of her bed. The curtains blocked out the starlight at night and trapped the heat from the sun during the day. It kept the room warm when warmth was needed and cool when coolness was. It was a good room.

The bedroom could have been considered large for one person. There was lots of play space on the circular rug in the middle of the floor. It may have been too small for two people. The only other bedroom was her parents'. Which meant she would soon have to share the room that had been hers and hers alone since forever. Did babies sleep in their parents' room for a while after they were born, so their mother could keep an eye on them? How often did they wake up in the night? Would Sheila hear the crying and wake up too?

Having a brother or sister might be fun. All her friends who had siblings talked about them a lot. It might be nice to have a friend around all the time too, even if Sheila would be so much older. She felt a smile creep its way onto her face. She thought she would be a good sister.

But then she thought about something else, and the smile fell away. She sat up in bed. Suddenly she was sweating under her arms. Visions of the handsy man from one of the drop-offs for her father rushed through her mind.

Sheila was strong. She was not afraid of the men her father had her meet for him. She could handle it. It was her responsibility to their family. That was what her father said. If she was thirteen, that meant she only had four or five years left of school—and that included upper secondary school.

Sheila was eleven the first time her father packed her backpack. She thought about that timing with her new brother or sister. When Sheila was ready to leave for university, her brother or sister would still be a few years out from running favors for their father. But what if he started them early, once Sheila was gone, to keep it going? Maybe that was why he was so happy earlier. Maybe that was why he thought it was good news—his business had just been blessed with another decade, unexpectedly. It made sense why he might see it that way.

What if her brother or sister was not as strong as her, though? If they were younger than she was when she started, that would all but certainly be the case. What if they were afraid? What if something went wrong? Her thoughts made her scared. It was a big sister's job to protect her little brother or sister, and that was what Sheila was becoming. Which meant it was her job to protect them, to make sure they did not have to do what she did. She still did not know what exactly it was she was doing for her father, but she knew it was dangerous—that was why her father gave her the special combinations each time.

What could she do about it? The baby was not even born yet, so she had some time to think about it and come up with a plan. She did not know what that meant yet, or what that might look like. But one thing she knew for sure, the more she considered everything, was that having a brother or sister was definitely not good news. That was yet another thing her father had been wrong about.

# CHAPTER FIVE

*Present day.* Sheila was asleep on the sofa with a throw pillow nestled in her arms. Blackness was all Randolph could see through the window behind her head. Sheila still wore the burgundy cocktail dress she put on for dinner. The ankle straps on her heels were undone. One of them dangled from her toes, swaying back and forth along with the motion of the waves.

Randolph sat on the bed with his back against the headboard. Despite the early hour—the clock told him it was nearly two o'clock—he was nowhere near sleep. His mind raced. Dinner with Sheila had not gone as he expected. The passion she spoke with, the emotion of it, hit him square in the chest like a human freight train. At times she cried, others she clenched her jaw with anger and frustration and disgust. Her vulnerabilities and deep, dark insecurities about where she came from and who she was forced to become were not fabrications. Only a fool could have thought that.

Their conversation stretched long into the night. Everything was on the table now between them—or at least Randolph hoped it was everything. He was not sure how much more he could handle. He felt overwhelmed with all the information as it was.

On one hand, he felt justified in trusting her now, more than ever. On the other, he felt terrified—not just for himself, but for her. What she was up against was something far bigger than herself, and more powerful—and worth more than any one life.

He could not do nothing. This was all so far out of his league and beyond his expertise, but he could never live with himself should Sheila lose. What if something happened to her? He did not ask, but he imagined she would not be the first. He had to help. What that meant exactly, he could not say right now.

This was crazy. All of it—what happened in the supermarket; what happened with Patricia; being with Sheila now; being in the depths of this situation. He could not understand it, how he got here. But here he was, and now he had to figure it out.

He reached across his body and stretched for the water bottle on the nightstand. As soon as his fingers touched it, he knew it was empty. He tried to swallow but failed. Dehydration was coming on strong. He checked the clock again and sighed—it had only been four minutes. How was it that time passed so slowly when experiencing insomnia, yet it moved so fast all other times? One day your child was in diapers, the next he was off to college, then married with his own. Time was one of life's most infuriating phenomenon.

The mattress squeaked as he shifted his weight and swung his legs over the edge of the bed. He grimaced and shot a glance to Sheila, who remained asleep and undisturbed. His feet found a pair of slip-ons. On the way to the door, he swiped one of the keycards from the counter and pocketed it, then slipped into the hallway. The door clicked behind him.

Far above him, the party was still ongoing. He heard laughter and felt the rumble of the bass through his chest. He recalled seeing a sign about an all-night bash to celebrate the final night onboard, which explained what was happening. While he admired those who still had that type of energy at this time of night, he was not jealous. If he had it his way, he would be deep into a long sleep cycle right now.

In his mind, he traced the quickest route to one of the shops where he could find more water. Left, he thought—no, right. He went right. A woman squealed with laughter in the arms of her man, who gracefully ran down the corridor in his direction. The man put the woman down and fumbled around in his pocket, one hand on the door handle. The woman nuzzled his neck and began unbuttoning his shirt, moving her lips downward as she did. Randolph averted his eyes and picked up his pace until he passed them. He heard the woman squeal again as he rounded the corner.

A shop was not far ahead. He greeted the worker with a smile and grabbed as many waters as could fit in his hands, then brought them to the counter. He gave the lady his room number and scooped them up again and left. Back at the room, he tucked a bottle under his chin and found the key, then pressed inside. Sheila was still asleep, except now, both heels had fallen. He smiled at her.

He drained one of the bottles and lined the others next to the coffee grounds. Surprisingly, he did not have to pee. Not yet, anyway. It would not be long, he knew. His eyes suddenly felt heavy. The exhaustion had finally come with a vengeance, and the urge to close his eyes was strong. He grabbed one of the folded blankets from the edge of the bed and draped it over Sheila's exposed ankles. She moaned and shifted her weight, then grabbed the edge of the blanket and pulled it toward her neck.

Randolph smiled again. He was doing the right thing, being here. With her. Sheila was not a bad person—he knew that for sure now. Some of those other things—some of the choices she made, the way she acted sometimes, the little white lies—were just flaws that every living, breathing person had too. Randolph was not perfect either. He drove his wife to hate him so much, she wanted him dead. Nobody would look good under a microscope if only their mistakes were visible. Sheila deserved a second chance. Maybe they did too.

Randolph flipped off his shoes and fell onto the bed. Sleep was finally on the horizon. He reached over and switched off the light, enveloping them in darkness. His breathing slowed. He felt himself drifting.

Then he heard a voice. A mumble.

"Sheila?" he whispered.

There was no answer at first. Then: "Don't," the voice mumbled again. "Please don't."

Randolph shot up and switched the light back on, his heart rate quickening. Sheila remained asleep on the sofa, but her lips were twitching.

"Please don't," she mumbled again. "No, please don't."

Randolph was suddenly no longer tired.

# CHAPTER SIX

*Present day.* Benji was up all night, because he most always was. It was his overactive mind's fault. Gary and Patricia had called it a night many hours ago, which left Benji to his own accord to watch the monitors for any activity. So far, there had been none. He expected the others to arrive at the office any time now.

His latest text to Justice remained unanswered. He picked up and put down his phone hundreds of times over the past few hours to look at the screen, even though the volume was turned up and the vibration was on; he would have heard it if it went off. The battery was running low. It was almost 10 a.m., which meant it was the middle of the night in Fiji, just a different day. Ahead or behind, he could not wrap his mind around. Either way, he knew Justice was likely asleep, but still. He missed her.

Admitting that surprised him. He rarely felt smitten the way he did with her, but there was something about her that he found addicting. He thought about it a lot but was yet to put a finger on what it was. Whatever it was, he wanted more of it, of her. Needed it. Craved it. She was his new drug of choice. The prospect of being with her soon drove him, kept him motivated even when the maps on his monitors were devoid of red dots.

The trick was how to fill his time. There was no weed. Pornography bored him. The databases Gary hooked him up with were only accessible when Gary was around. Gary did not want him snooping in places he did not belong, he said. Benji could not fault him for that. A bored, curious mind could do a lot of things that probably should not be done. Like build a pipe bomb, for example.

Randolph's phone was being tracked. Sheila's passports were too. With so many aliases, there was no saying which one she was using these days, so Gary tracked them all. Made sense. But it did not seem to be working, because none of them had registered. At least not yet.

Benji went through Randolph's records again. On the flight to Fiji, Gary had Benji slip a tracking device into Randolph's phone, which was far easier than Benji thought. Most phones these days had a nonremovable battery, but Gary guessed right about Randolph, who had not been carrying the latest tech in his pocket. Which meant Benji could pop out the battery, slip the chip underneath, and put it all back together in a matter of a few seconds. Easy as pie. Randolph had, apparently, not bothered taking it out. Slipped his mind, perhaps.

From Benji's perspective, the activity on Randolph's phone was not unusual. Once they got back from Fiji, Randolph went straight home to Cedar Rapids, Iowa, and all indications were that he stayed there. After being off the grid for a short time, he did not venture far after that, primarily just around town. That lasted for two weeks. Benji now knew that at that point, Randolph packed all his belongings, rented a moving truck, and drove halfway across the country to Green River, Utah, to visit his son— with an unexpected visit to see his ex-wife in prison on the way. Utah, Benji understood. But Randolph visiting his ex-wife, the woman who hired Benji to kill him, was not something that made any sense at all. Unfinished business or closure, maybe, or conversations that needed to be had. Benji would never understand the dynamic of having spent so much time with another person and having so much shared history, so he would not pretend to try to. He brushed it off.

After Green River, Gary got a hit on Sheila in Salt Lake City—also in Utah—so the three of them met up there, and were then sent to Grand Junction, Colorado. Was that where it started? Benji could not help but doubt it being a coincidence. Randolph was in Green River while Sheila was in Salt Lake City, a mere three hours away—or Grand Junction, Colorado, which was even closer. Of all the places Sheila could have been, why there? That perplexed him. Be that as it may, Benji did not think Randolph acted abnormally in Salt Lake City. If anything, he was angry about being there, irritated about being away from his family in Green River. If he and Sheila were in cahoots, Benji still failed to see it.

Perhaps the most baffling circumstance of all was what happened next. There was an arranged meeting place where they could trap and capture Sheila, but she never showed, even though she set it up. That night, at the hotel, Randolph disappeared. Benji had been to his room not long before and suspected nothing. The last ping on his phone occurred at a coordinate only a few miles from the hotel they stayed at, and it had not moved in more than two weeks. Two weeks! How was that even possible?

It was unfathomable. Either Randolph was dead or he ditched his phone. The idea of him even thinking to get rid of the phone made no sense. From what Benji knew about him and observed when they were together, the man hardly knew how to use the phone, never mind had the presence of mind to be aware of the technological capabilities it held. For that, all signs pointed to him working with someone.

Sheila. It had to be.

Right?

Who else could it be?

But why?

The whole situation frustrated Benji. He was at his wits end with it. Justice was not responding, his insomnia had returned ever since being home, and he felt restless. He sighed. The phone pinged, but only to remind him to plug it in before its battery died.

He needed some air. There were no windows in the office, and he had not seen natural light in he was not sure how long. Days? A week? He was not positive what day of the week it was. He stood up and stretched his back, felt it pop. Pangs of hunger rushed through him as his stomach growled. Snacks. He needed snacks. He remembered seeing a vending machine at one point the last time he left the room. He shoved his hands in his pockets and came up empty. Hopefully the snacks were free.

He leaned forward and scooped the empty cup off the desk. Water, he knew for sure, was definitely free. Just as he turned to leave, something flashed on his monitor. He did a double-take and turned back. His vision must have been blurry, he thought, having been looking at the screen for so long. It was just his eyes playing a trick on him. He rubbed them. When he looked again, it was still there.

A red dot.

A single red dot.

Benji kept his eyes on the monitor and plopped back down in the chair. Snacks now seemed less important, the hunger pangs gone just as quickly as they came. One red dot. Not two. That was unexpected. He grabbed the mouse and hovered over the new dot. Sheila. It was Sheila. Where was Randolph? Did that mean they were not together? He felt justified in his feelings about it, about Randolph—he was not conspiring with Sheila. But then he remembered Randolph's phone in Utah and how it had not moved. If it was ditched, that could mean he and Sheila were indeed together. Either way, there was no proof. Benji was torn.

Quickly, he snatched his phone and dialed Gary, keeping his eyes on the monitor. It rang and rang and rang, then went to voicemail. Benji tossed the phone back on the desk in frustration. Before something changed, he took a screenshot of his monitor so he could show Gary later. He kept his eyes glued to the screen.

Just then, the office door creaked open. Gary said something Benji missed, then Patricia laughed. Benji's attention was elsewhere.

"We brought doughnuts," Gary said.

"Dibs on the jelly," Patricia said.

Benji sensed someone behind him.

"Got anything for me?" It was Gary.

"You'd know the answer to that question if you picked up your phone," Benji said.

"What, did you call?"

"Look," Benji said, ignoring the question. He pointed at the red dot on the monitor.

"When was this?" Gary said, timid excitement in his voice.

"Just a few minutes ago."

"You got something?" Patricia added through muffled chewing.

"We got her," Gary said.

"My god. Both of them?"

"Just her."

"What about Randolph?"

"They're together."

"How do you know?"

"I just know. Trust me."

The doubt rang through Benji's mind, but he did not say anything. Maybe Gary knew something he did not. Very likely.

"You can't hide from me," Gary said to no one in particular in a crooked tone. "I've got you now."

# CHAPTER SEVEN

*Twelve years ago.* Sheila's little sister was born on a sweltering summer day. She remembered waking up in the night to the sound of her mother wailing in pain. Sheila shot up in her bed in fear, her hands balling the blankets. Underneath the door, the light in the hallway flipped on, and she heard lots of commotion. Her father's voice was raised in a panicked tone, though she could not understand the words. A minute later, her mother was no longer crying, and her father's voice was back to normal.

Sheila found that the scariest part.

What was happening?

After more commotion and another minute, the door to her room creaked open and her father walked in, fully dressed but looking disheveled silhouetted against the illuminated hallway.

"Sheila, your mother and me need to go to the hospital now," he said.

Sheila flipped the blankets off her and swung her legs over the side of the bed. She could be dressed and in the car in thirty seconds.

"No, not you."

She stopped, confused.

"You stay. Keep an eye on the house. Can you do that for me?"

Sheila felt hurt, unwanted, but nodded in response to her father.

"That's my good girl."

Then the door closed again and Sheila was left in the darkness, very much awake and very much alone.

• • • • •

It was the longest, most agonizing day of Sheila's life. Since it was summertime and school was out, she had nowhere to be, nothing to do, nothing to occupy her mind. When the night turned into day, she finally got out of bed despite being awake before and got dressed. She poured herself cereal for breakfast and brushed her teeth afterward like she always did.

As the day progressed, so did the heat. The house felt like a sauna, hotter and stickier than ever. Upstairs in her bedroom was even worse. She spent much of the day on the living room sofa with a book and an oscillating fan, but was unable to focus long enough to read much. For lunch, she ate a banana and a bowl of kiwi, but that was it. Warmed leftover rice for dinner. Her appetite was all but lost.

When night fell again, the heat relented and gave way to a moderate breeze, which was such a relief. She opened all the windows upstairs and cracked the ones downstairs to let the trapped warmth escape. At her usual bedtime, she went upstairs and crawled into her bed, but lay awake, unable to turn her mind off. She was worried about her mother. She did not feel scared to be home alone; her father had put her through more dangerous situations after school than she could ever experience at home. She was not afraid of men breaking into the house. What she was afraid of was losing her mother.

Sometime in the middle of the night, or possibly early the next morning, Sheila was awoken by a rattling noise downstairs.

Her chest fluttered at the sound—but not because she was scared, just startled. She popped out of bed and ran to the window and pulled back the curtain. Her father's car was in the driveway. She grabbed her robe and bolted downstairs.

The first person she saw was her father, who looked just as disheveled as he had in the silhouette of the hallway the last time she saw him, just worse. Now, his hair was rumpled in the back and his shirt was untucked. He turned and she saw his face and the deep, dark bags under his eyes. It looked like he had not slept. He held up a finger to his lips when their eyes connected.

Sheila nodded and kept moving down the stairs with a hand tightly gripping the railing. She moved slowly so to avoid making a noise. Once her father moved aside and pulled the door open wider, in stepped her mother—tenderly, slowly, with tiny steps. Sheila's heart raced in anticipation of what would come next.

Wrapped up in her mother's arms, cocooned within a white blanket, was a tiny, adorable baby wearing a knit hat. Sheila gasped aloud. Both her parents shushed her. Sheila covered her mouth but kept moving, following her mother into the living room, where her mother sat. Her father disappeared into his office and closed the door. Sheila stood in the doorway of the living room, her back against the frame, unsure what to say or do or how to act. This was all new to her. It was then her mother looked up and smiled at her.

"Want to meet her, sweetheart?" her mother asked.

"Her?"

"It's a girl." Her mother smiled again. "You have a little sister."

Sheila felt something roll inside her belly—butterflies, she wondered. She had heard about the phenomenon but never knew what it meant until that moment. Her everything trembled just a little, mostly with excitement. With her eyes locked on the tiny baby, she walked toward her mother and sat next to her. Their hips touched.

As if her mother could read her mind, she said, "Put your arms like this," showing her.

Sheila mimicked what her mother was doing and looked down to make sure it looked the same.

"Good," her mother said. Then, ever so gingerly as if the baby were fragile, she pulled the baby across her body and placed it into Sheila's arms, blanket intact.

Sheila's breath caught in her throat. Her eyes were glued on the precious, human-like creature in her arms. She had not seen many babies before, certainly not up close, never mind held one. It did not seem real. The baby's eyes were closed, purple veins snaking her eyelids. She smelled so fresh, so clean, so new. Sheila was in awe, and completely in love.

"You're a big sister now," her mother said quietly, dropping a soft hand on her elbow.

And she was. She really was.

"What's her name?" Sheila whispered, afraid to wake the baby.

"Minka."

Minka. She liked that.

"Minka. Baby Minka." Sheila smiled at baby Minka. "Hi, baby Minka. I'm your big sister. I'm going to take care of you forever. I'll never let anything happen to you. I'll protect you from the bad things. I promise."

And it was a promise she intended to keep.

# CHAPTER EIGHT

*Present day.* An alarm clock was not necessary. With all the chaos on board—doors opening and closing in the corridor; people shuffling in and out, bags smacking and being tossed against the walls, whether intentionally or not; voices galore—it was impossible not to wake. Randolph's eyes were heavy when he did. A dull pressure lingered. He needed more water.

Within the hour, he and Sheila were dressed and packed, their bellies full of simple carbohydrates. Randolph swallowed a couple of preventive acetaminophens, downed another bottle of water, and went into the bathroom. He held himself over the bowl, pushing from deep inside his gut. The pressure in his prostate was not relieved much as he dribbled, even when he tried forcing it. If he pushed too hard it would burn, so he did not. He knew the drill; he would be back in a few minutes to finish emptying his bladder. All of those things were on his list of talking points to address with his doctor, the next time he went.

The next hour was a blur. He and Sheila stood in line with hundreds of other happy, smiling travelers. Some of them laughed, others hid their hangovers behind the shade of dark sunglasses. One woman's shoulders were so red, she could have had permanent burns. Another was browned everywhere except around her eyes, where Randolph assumed the cucumbers once were. While the vibes were of stress-fee relaxation, there was an irrefutable aura of reality lingering over the crowd. Life was on hold for the past two weeks, for everyone onboard. All their problems at home would still be there when they returned. The furnace would still leak; the seal on the freezer would still need replacing; the windows would still be drafty. The fun was over. Back to work on Monday for many. For others, it meant picking the kids up from their grandma's and settling back into the monotonous routine of suburban life. It was the one thing everyone knew but nobody spoke of; real-life waited on the other side of the gate.

With bags in tow, the line moved onward. Down the gangway, onto the dock, past the crew, many of whom shook hands and laughed and pocketed tips. A few accepted hugs.

Randolph mostly kept his head down and let Sheila lead the way. He knew she had a plan. Her advice to him was to not ask many questions so she would not have to lie; she was tired of all the lies. He was too. Which meant if he wanted details, all he had to do was ask. But as he had learned over the years, sometimes the less he knew the better. It was like seeing things you did not want to see—once you saw them, you could not unsee them. Some minds were not strong enough to push those things aside and truly forget. He suspected his was not. So for now, at least, he would try to relinquish control and let Sheila do what she had to do, what she was good at. She had proven to be a pro.

They approached a massive structure with large windows and a rounded overhanging roof. Under the overhang hung a sign with giant blue letters that read: Pier 2 Passenger Terminal. Randolph followed Sheila through the sliding doors. It was like a tiny airport inside—people everywhere, illuminated signs, long lines near the bathrooms. They hurried through the crowd.

Back outside on the other end, Sheila finally pulled up on the sidewalk. She dropped her bag and slid two fingers into her mouth. A booming whistle screeched and her hand shot up. A cab pulled up not long after.

"This is it, Randolph," she said to him. "You've had time to think about everything we've talked about. Now's the time to make your decision. Just say the word and we can split up right now, and you'll never hear from me again."

"I trust you."

"You can take this cab and I'll flag the next."

"Did you not hear what I said?"

"The airport's about six miles from here. I can hang out here for a bit, give you time to get ahead."

Randolph dropped a hand on Sheila's forearm. She immediately tensed. He kept his hand there, said nothing. A few seconds passed. He felt the tension fall off her. She looked at him then. Her eyes were not wet, but Randolph saw something deep inside them that told him just as much as if they were. This was real for her. As much as she would do what she had to do with or without him, she really wanted someone there with her. Which made sense, that was a natural reaction—the longing for companionship. But not just any someone; she wanted Randolph there. She wanted him.

"I trust you," he repeated. "And I'm going with you."

She held his gaze for a few seconds longer. The edges of her mouth widened just a smidge, but it was enough. Randolph understood. They climbed into the back of the cab. Together.

"Airport," Sheila said to the driver.

"You got it," the driver said with an unrecognizable accent, then off they went.

. . . . .

Daniel K. Inouye International Airport was surrounded by a magnificent oceanic horizon and cultural gardens native to the island. Hawaiian culture was ripe within the gardens, complete with flowing waterways and island sculptures and exotic ferns. Randolph spotted weeping willows and pine and bamboo trees, and an amazing pavilion with a yellow curved roof housing resting benches. If not for what was to come, it could have been the most serene place on the planet. If only he had the time to sit back and enjoy it.

He did not.

"Ready?" Sheila said, pulling him from his stupor.

He shook himself and looked around. They stood in the entryway of the airport. He was not sure how they got there, exactly, or how long they had been standing there. People swarmed like bees. Voices and loudspeaker notifications and babies crying and a strange buzzing noise from somewhere overhead overwhelmed him. He realized his bag hung from his shoulder, although he could not remember getting out of the cab or entering the airport. He was spiraling.

"You okay?" Sheila asked him.

"I think I need to sit down."

She hooked his arm and pulled him toward the nearest bench, where they sat. He heard a zipper then saw a bottle of water, which Sheila shoved into his hand. He took it and twisted the cap off and pushed the bottle toward his lips.

"You good?"

He swallowed hard and felt the lukewarm water rush through him. His head spun, but he felt a little better. "Just give me a few minutes to rest. I'll be all right."

"Will you be okay to hang here for a bit?"

"Where are you going?"

She raised her eyebrows but did not say anything, as if waiting for him to figure it out on his own. Which he did. He remembered their conversation from dinner, and it all clicked.

"Oh, right," he said. "Right."

She nodded.

"Yeah, go. I'll be good."

"I'll be back soon." She offered him a tight smile, then stood up and walked away. The crowd swallowed her whole. Randolph quickly lost sight of her.

He had not been counting, but he figured it was about a half hour before she returned. By then, the water bottle was emptied and he felt better, just hungry. The bagel from the morning had worn off. Frankly, he was surprised it lasted that long.

"Hey," Sheila said.

"Hey."

She handed him a blue notebook-like pad. A passport. Complete with the United States seal. He ran his finger along the edge. It looked, and felt, genuine. And that made him feel intensely anxious. What if it did not work? What would they do to him? He looked up at Sheila.

"You said you trust me, right?"

He nodded.

"Good." She sat down next to him and placed a hand on his knee. "It'll work. I promise. I've done this more times than I care to admit."

He believed and trusted her. At this point, he had no choice but to. He looked down and opened the passport. Inside was a photo of him. A headshot. Where Sheila got it from, he had no idea, nor did he care to ask.

"Wilbur Monroe from Wyoming," he read. "Wilbur?"

"Hey, you can't pick and choose with things like this."

"Who are you?"

She slipped a hand under her blouse and fidgeted. When it came out, there was a passport in it.

"What else you got in there?"

Sheila laughed. "Some women wear padded bras, I buy a size or two bigger so I have extra room. They're not that big, you know that."

Randolph did not know how to respond to that. What she said was true, but he loved her the way she was; nothing could change that. He looked away and blushed. Sheila playfully shoved him. The gesture lightened the mood.

"Judith Kleinman."

He looked at her. "What?"

"Judith Kleinman," she repeated. Then she opened the passport in her hand and looked down. "From Kansas. That's me. I used it once before, but that was years ago. I don't even remember what for."

Randolph nodded. The explanation was good enough for him. "Well, shall we?"

He took a deep breath and stood. "I guess this is it."

Sheila stood too and hooked his arm. "C'mon. We've got this." They headed for customs.

When it was their turn, Sheila went first. Her bag was opened and rummaged through without issue. The customs agent took her passport and looked back and forth between it, his computer monitor, and Sheila. Then he handed it back.

Randolph was up. His heart was in his throat, and he noticed how shaky he was as he struggled to unzip his bag for the agent. Perspiration beaded on his forehead. He felt warm. He sensed the agent staring at him, but he refused to look up and make eye contact. He could only imagine how guilty he must have looked.

"Passport?"

"Huh?"

"Passport, Sir."

"Oh, right." Randolph reached into his back pocket. His wallet came with the passport, which he pushed toward the agent but dropped it during the transfer. He quickly bent over and scooped it up as if there were a five-second rule. Then he nearly tossed it at the agent and placed his wallet on the countertop.

The agent went through the same process as he had with Sheila—opened the passport, looked between the photo and Randolph's face, then glanced at his monitor. It took forever, it seemed to Randolph, longer than it had with Sheila. What was wrong? Was he caught? What would happen to him now? Was security on their way?

"Here you go, Sir," the agent said, handing the passport across the desk.

Randolph used his wrist to swipe his forehead before taking the passport back. He smiled at the agent and turned away.

"Wait!" the agent said, and Randolph's heart fell.

This was it. Just when he thought he was in the clear . . .

"Your wallet."

Randolph turned toward the agent and there it was: his wallet, folded up on the countertop, precisely where he left it. If the agent picked it up and saw Randolph's real ID inside, Randolph was screwed. His scam would be over before it started. He did not know if he could handle the pressure of it all, which was quickly mimicking a noose around his neck and trying its darndest to suffocate him.

The agent did pick up the wallet. He grabbed it but kept it closed, and extended his arm toward Randolph. Randolph stepped back and took it, and smiled again. He wondered if the agent could tell he was teetering through what he knew was a toothy grin.

"Have a nice flight, Mr. Monroe."

*Who?*

Oh, right. That was him. He was Mr. Wilbur Monroe from Wyoming. How would he ever remember that? He was not cut out for this.

"Thank you," Randolph said. Then he turned away.

A few paces up ahead, he fell into step with Sheila. Sweat drenched him.

"You've got to relax, Randolph. Deep breaths."

"I think I'm going to throw up."

"The hard part's over. We're fine."

"No, really, I think I'm going to throw up."

His stomach twisted and gurgled. Thankfully, a men's room was just up ahead on the left, and there was no line. Randolph dropped his bag where he was and took off running toward the lineless restroom. He made it into the nearest stall just in time and hurled. And he hurled a lot.

# CHAPTER NINE

*Present day.*

"Judith Kleinman," Gary said to the room. "I know that name." A box of file folders sat on the edge of the table, papers scattered everywhere. He rummaged through the chaos, frantically searching for something unknown.

Benji watched him with bewilderment at how highly unorganized Gary was, yet at the same time seeming to know precisely where to find whatever he was after. For such an important guy, supposedly, with an important job, his personality did not seem to fit. But what did Benji know? Patricia lingered over Gary's shoulder like a shadow, crumbs from her doughnut littering the carpet, a nuisance among rats.

"Got it!" Gary exclaimed as he held up a manila folder over his head as if it were a trophy.

Patricia squealed with delight in response. Benji peeked over his shoulder at the monitor, where the single red dot blinked. The dot had not moved, which meant Sheila had not either.

Gary swiped his hand across the table and pushed some of the scattered papers out of the way, some of which fell to the floor with the slow-motion movement of a feather. The folder in his hand flipped open and Gary leaned in to get a closer look. Patricia finished the doughnut and creeped forward. Even Benji's curiosity was piqued enough to step in too, to check it out.

"Judith Kleinman," Gary read aloud, "born in Kansas. Aged twenty-two years. Father, aged fifty. Mother, deceased. No siblings. Clean record, not even a parking ticket. Graduate of Emporia State University. Studied Sociology. Works as a freelance life coach in Oklahoma. Current address unknown. How convenient?"

"Never heard of her," Patricia said.

"That's because she doesn't exist."

"Excuse me?"

"It's one of Sheila's many aliases. Seldom used. According to my records, only once. Four years ago. Flew from Stillwater, Oklahoma, to Cancun. Never came back."

"Why would she use a fake ID just once four years ago and not again until now?"

"If there's one thing I've learned while tracking her, it's to not try to figure her out. As counterproductive as that might sound. But it's true. Trying to predict what she'll do next or why will just leave you pissed off. Trust me on that. I'd know."

Benji did not know what to think.

"But why she used this alias," Gary said, folding his arms and looking into space, "is befuddling. I must admit, I'm surprised by it. Either she's gotten lazy, or we just got supremely lucky. Like we should play the lottery lucky."

Benji turned and looked over his shoulder again to verify the dot was still on the monitor. It was.

"The way I see it," Gary said, "one of two things just happened. One, we're being setup. Possible, I admit. Or two—and if it's door number two, then halle-fucking-lujah—she just made her first critical mistake. And it's about damn time. Everyone gets caught eventually—I'm talking everyone. Even Whitey got caught. Took damn near twenty years, but they got him. They always get their guy. Which is why I knew I'd get her—I just knew it. It was only a matter of time."

Patricia shuffled her feet and moved in close to Gary. She said, "So, what do we do now?"

"Let me make a few phone calls and verify some details first. Then we'll go from there."

With that, Gary pulled out his phone and left the room, the door softly clicking closed behind him. Leaving Benji alone with Randolph's ex-wife, someone with whom he had become very familiar with himself. It did not even take five seconds before she spoke.

"Hello, lover."

Benji groaned. "Don't. Just don't."

"What's the matter, lover?" She stepped toward him.

Benji backed away. "Haven't you done enough damage already? Just let the guy be."

"Who?"

"Come on, you know who I'm talking about."

She scoffed. "Randolph. Why are you so loyal to him all of a sudden? Did you forget that you're not exactly innocent?"

"That's the difference between you and me. I regret getting involved. I know what I did was wrong. But you . . . you'll never own up to it. You'll keep laying blame on everyone else."

"If you're such a saint then why are you here?"

"Why are you?"

She smiled. "Same reason as you. To save my own ass."

Benji did not know what to say. Ultimately, Patricia was right. How different were they, really?

"I just hope you're not dumb enough to screw this up," she said. "If you try something stupid and this backfires, you know we're both going back, right?"

She meant behind bars. That reality hovered over him like a dark cloud. It was so true. "What makes you think Gary's not going to double-cross us and screw us both anyway?"

"If I'm being honest, I can't say for sure that he won't. Maybe he will. But it's worth the risk. What's the alternative?"

"So that's it? You're here just to save yourself?"

"Aren't you?"

No response.

"Listen, I know you think you know Randolph and you think you know me, but you really don't," she said. "Maybe I haven't said it out loud, but that doesn't mean I don't regret what happened. And as much as you want to change what we did, you can't. Life doesn't work that way. All we can do is move on and make the best of it. So when Gary came knocking, asking if I knew where Randolph might have gone, I seized the opportunity. Any shot I got, I'm going to take it. Same as you. Same as all of us. Anyone with a brain, anyway."

In some ways, Benji respected that. In others, he thought it sounded like complete bullshit. Unfortunately, the truth did not matter in this situation. All that mattered was helping Gary since he was the one holding all the cards, pulling all the strings. What would happen after would be what it would be; it was out of their hands.

Benji did not like the odds.

"Can we move on, or what?" Patricia said. "Work together to do what we have to do and hope for the best? Then afterward, you never have to see me again. And it would be a whole hell of a lot easier to coexist if you stopped looking at me like I'm the only guilty person in this room."

"Fine."

"Fine as in you're going to stop acting like a dick?"

Across the room, the door clicked.

"Am I interrupting something?" Gary said, now back. He looked between them.

"Nothing at all," Patricia said. "We're fine here."

"Good, because it's time to get back to work." Gary walked toward the table and sat down. He grabbed his laptop and opened it.

Benji followed Patricia to where Gary was.

"They're pulling the CCTV footage now," Gary said. "I'm expecting it to come through any second."

As if by magic, Gary's computer pinged. He quickly clicked on the new message and opened the attachment. A video played.

Benji was not sure what he was looking for, but his eyes were glued to the screen. The footage rotated through different angles, seemingly at nothing. Then he saw it. From up above, a woman crossed into frame. She was alone. A few seconds later, a man fell in step with her. A few seconds after that, the man broke out in what looked like a sprint.

Then the footage paused.

Benji looked at Gary, whose face was unusually close to the screen.

"May I?" Benji asked. He felt all eyes on him. Gary stood back. Benji leaned in and used the trackpad to drive to the navigation menu, where he zoomed in and blew up the footage. When he did, the faces of the two people they were watching became crystal clear.

Them. It was them.

# CHAPTER TEN

*Eleven years ago.* Sheila loved being a big sister. Baby Minka slept in their parents' room for the first six months of her life. Which, in retrospect, Sheila thought was helpful for the transition of being an only child to having to share her space. The bedroom felt crowded once Minka slept in there too. The crib was compact and fit snuggly against the wall where Sheila's smaller shelf of books once was. The shelf went to the attic and Sheila's books went into a box under her bed. She did not like being unable to look at them and read the spines, but at least they were easily accessible. The sacrifice was not that great; they were just books, even if she liked them.

Minka stole most of their mother's attention, but that was okay; it was just an observation. Sheila still had her afternoons during the school year where she would sit with her mother in the kitchen while dinner was being made. Honestly, that was enough for her. She was fifteen years old and could not have cared less about spending less time with her mother. By then, her father was busier than ever and often came home after dark or just before bedtime. Sometimes not at all. She remembered not seeing him for an entire week one winter, which actually was nice. When he was gone, that meant she would not have any drop-offs to make after school, so she could act like the other teenagers at school did. That occasionally meant going to a friend's house after school or joining a study group or casually learning the play to violin. She could not fully commit to joining the band, though, because she never knew exactly when her father would need her after school. It was her responsibility to the family, after all.

As much as the distance grew between her and her parents, she felt the opposite with Minka. She found herself missing Minka during the day and was anxious to see her when she got home most of the time—in a good way. Which was why she seldom stayed out beyond dinnertime. Doing so meant she might not see her sister before she was put down to sleep. Even during the nights when Minka was fussy and the hallway light woke Sheila as her mother went back and forth between bedrooms, Sheila enjoyed having her sister around. She was someone to talk to, even if she did not talk back. Minka was the best listener.

Minka grew up so fast. Her legs seemed to get longer every day, her awareness sharper as she took in the world around her with wide, unblinking eyes. Before long, she was crawling across the floor and touching things she was not supposed to, slipping trinkets into her mouth that did not belong there. Sheila soon learned to put anything that might tempt Minka—which was just about everything—on top of the shelf that remained, or inside the drawers of her bureau, or taking them out of the bedroom altogether.

One day when she came home from school, her mother had put together a plastic playpen with transparent netting and an overhanging sensory toy that made lots of noise. Minka was set up with it in the living room while their mother busied in the kitchen. Sheila hoped that meant the playpen could go upstairs sometimes too so Sheila could put some of her trinkets back on display, but she never asked because she did not want to seem ungrateful for their family.

Another time, following a long weekend where their mother felt unwell, Minka was especially fussy during the night. Their father was home but preoccupied in his office as he usually was. Minka cried for minutes and minutes—which felt like far more than that to Sheila—and still neither their mother nor father came in to check on the baby. As the wails intensified and Sheila's hope for a good sleep before the exam she had at school the next day was all but forgotten, she tossed the sheet aside and walked over to the crib.

Minka looked up at her with wet eyes, red cheeks, and a runny nose. Sheila flipped the light on to get a better look at what she was doing and thought she saw what the problem was. Minka's pacifier had fallen out of her crib and onto the floor. Shelia bent down and scooped it up and gently pushed it into Minka's mouth, who immediately pushed it back out with her tongue. Minka wailed ever harder.

Moments later, Sheila felt a prick on her finger. She looked down and noticed that, somehow, Minka had grabbed Sheila's finger and slipped it into her mouth. Sheila wiggled her finger inside Minka's mouth and felt the sharp edge of what she assumed was Minka's first tooth popping through. Minka sucked on Sheila's fingertip, and before long her eyes were closed and the tears dried up.

Sheila watched in awe with a rush of emotions—from an everlasting love to relief that the noise had stopped—as Minka snuggled with her tiny blanket while sucking on Sheila's finger. Sheila waited a couple of minutes before trying to pull her finger out, but Minka would not let go. Afraid to force it and injure her sister or wake her up, Sheila was resigned to the idea that she would spend the rest of the night that way.

The next morning, she awoke on the floor with a blanket draped over her. Minka was not in her crib. Sheila made her way downstairs and into the kitchen, where her mother spoon-fed Minka and her father buried his face in the newspaper.

"Good morning, sweetheart," her mother said the same way she always did. Nothing further. No acknowledgement of the evening before or expression of gratitude for stepping up even when it was not her job to do so.

When Sheila's eyes met with Minka's, her heart felt fuller than it ever had before. Minka cackled and stretched her arms for Sheila, who smiled and stepped toward her. She picked Minka up and was given the biggest tiny hug that was so intimate she could have cried. Minka rested her head on Sheila's shoulder as they rocked for a few seconds before their mother interrupted so to move the day along.

While neither one of her parents ever expressed their appreciation for Sheila that day, Minka did without ever saying a word—and she did not have to. Sheila could see it in her sweet eyes, feel it in her embrace.

From then on, things were different between Sheila and her parents, and she and Minka's bond grew stronger. Which made what happened next as gut-wrenching and emotionally devastating as Sheila would ever come to know. And it changed everything. Forever.

# CHAPTER ELEVEN

*Present day.* Randolph felt horrible—and not just physically. Knowingly committing multiple felonies and now becoming one of the types of people he once loathed ate at him more mentally than the physical reaction. He felt embarrassed and ashamed that it had come down to this, that his life had become this. But he also knew there was no turning back now. Even if he wanted to, it would be too late. Damage done.

He was all in.

He had a long time to think about it. They would be in the air over the Pacific Ocean for most of the day—roughly nine hours—not dissimilar to the flight he and Benji took to Fiji, just farther north.

Randolph thought about Benji, hoped he was managing. He wanted to reach out to let him know everything was going to work out, but he knew that would be careless; he simply could not do that so as to avoid putting everyone at risk. On one hand, he had concern about Benji's ability to cope and navigate his way through the shitstorm Gary was sure to put him through. On the other, Benji was an intelligent kid with more skills than he knew he had, so he would figure something out. Either way, Randolph had more pressing things to worry about—like himself, for once. He pushed the thoughts about Benji aside.

Bruce crossed his mind. Bruce and Maxwell and Janet. Those thoughts depressed him. The last time he and Bruce spoke was a blowout in Bruce's kitchen, where Randolph tried to defend himself and explain why he was still in contact with Gary and about how he went to Fiji with Benji. The conversation was delicate, as Randolph wanted his only son to understand, yet did not want to tell him too much so to keep him at an arm's length. The less he knew, the better. Unfortunately, Bruce did not understand and kicked Randolph out.

They had not spoken since, except for when Randolph sent him a text message with his new phone number—which, to no surprise, went unresponded to. As much as Randolph wanted to reach out again and again and again, he restrained himself. Bruce deserved space and time to process, especially with the new baby on the way. Bruce's wife Janet was seven, almost eight, months pregnant. Randolph had every intention of being there not only for the birth, but to be around to help afterward too. His plan had been to move to Utah to be nearby, to make a fresh start in a new place.

But it was not to be, thanks to Gary.

Randolph was still bitter about that. What kept him going was the hope that it might get better, that, once this was all over, there would still be time to reconnect and salvage his relationship with Bruce. Which in turn would mean a better, closer relationship with Maxwell and a solid foundation to start with the baby. Hope was all he had left. And he held onto it with everything he had.

After nine painstakingly long hours, the plane finally touched down. He and Sheila retrieved their bags, used the bathroom, made it through customs, used the bathroom again, and hailed a cab. Randolph's back ached from all the sitting. Or maybe he was just getting old.

The traffic leaving the airport was congested as they headed south past a Baptist church, an automotive repair shop, an apartment complex, then a sign for a water paradise. Later, there was a Shell gas station and a burger joint, which made Randolph realize how hungry he was; the snacks on the plane had not cut it. They did not stop, though. Onward. Another resort came into view shortly after they crossed the bridge. Downtown was typical of a downtown in any city in the States—department stores and eateries and hotels and a gift shop. Randolph could not even see the ocean from where they were, nestled in the heart of the city, despite it surrounding the island.

Sheila paid the cab driver, who surprisingly spoke excellent English. As the cab pulled away, their destination came into view. From the outside, it could have been a three-story house with two balconies and a garage on the ground level. No sign indicated otherwise. As they moved closer, a tiny inscription adjacent to the main door told him they were at a place called the Garden Palace, though it looked anything but. Modest. Far from extravagant.

In another word: genius.

The art of disappearing, Sheila explained over dinner their last night on the cruise ship, was blending in. Most people thought hiding in a remote location would be their best chance to stay hidden. But fewer people meant fewer visitors in these regions, which made outsiders stand out even more than they already did. Hiding in a city, however, often made more sense. Cities were packed with people, which meant it was near impossible to distinguish a local from an outsider. He thought that was counterproductive—more people meant better odds of being discovered. Right?

Wrong.

"You ever been to New York City or Chicago or any other major city?" she had asked over dinner while explaining the logic.

"Of course."

"You ever hear the phrase, 'New York City is the loneliest place in the world'?"

He had.

"I know from experience that it's true. Do you know how easy it is to blend in and become invisible in a place with eight million people? It's like being at a party in a room full of strangers. You might as well not even exist."

He could relate to that. The logic made perfect sense. Hide in plain sight. If you look and act like you belong, no one will look twice. So that was what they were going to do. Stay at a modest resort and keep their heads down, their profiles low. Meanwhile, Sheila would make contact and they would move forward with the next step. She made it sound so simple.

Naïve or not, Randolph believed it would be.

He had faith in Sheila. He believed in her and her plan. He had a logical, practical mind, and the plan checked all the boxes in his mind. His gut told him the plan was sound too. It also told him to trust what Sheila told him, do what she said, and be careful not to get in the way. When he combined his instincts with his brain, he felt good about where they were at. The rest of it—the challenges in his relationships back home, the legal trouble that could likely be bartered away if they did this the right way—would be resolved in time.

For now, he would sleep and await instructions from Sheila. The ball was in her court. There was nothing he could do but wait.

# CHAPTER TWELVE

*Present day.* Gary's grand plan was to wait it out, see what happened. Benji could not fathom that. They got digital verification about Sheila's whereabouts, so what were they waiting for? On top of that, the CCTV footage showed as clear as day that Randolph was with her. They were together, just as Gary predicted. So what was the hold up?

Benji tried to wrap his mind around what that meant for Randolph. Could it be true that he and Sheila had been conspiring the whole time? Benji just could not see it, despite the evidence sadly pointing in that direction. How far back did it go? Fiji? He ran through the scenarios in his mind and replayed them back. None of it made any sense. What was he missing?

According to the information Gary gathered, Sheila's alias and a man from Wyoming had adjoining seats and one-way tickets to Palau. Gary's ear was glued to his phone trying to figure out who this mystery man was and if he even existed. He needed confirmation before acting, he said. He was unconvinced of the CCTV footage; he claimed his eyes had played tricks on him in the past.

The worst part was waiting. It was not just that Gary needed more information about what they thought they saw, it was that it would take most of the day. Palau was closer to China than it was the United States, even Hawaii—which was where Sheila and her companion were before, who Benji knew from the CCTV footage was undoubtedly Randolph. A quick Google search told him the flight would take eight or nine hours.

That meant a lot of waiting, and a lot of doing nothing.

Luckily for Benji, those were two things he was an expert at.

He texted Justice just to say hello. She responded with a smiling emoji but said she could not talk because she had to go to work. Benji understood. He was happy she responded, at least. Justice was on his mind constantly.

Patricia left after a while. Something about needing to freshen up and get a bikini wax so she would be ready for island life. Frankly, Benji was glad to have her out of his space for a while. Whatever it took.

Gary was on the phone for a bit, then off, then back on. The keys on his laptop slammed as he pounded his fingers against them. Although curious, Benji thought better than to ask Gary what he was up to or if he could help. Hiding in the shadows and doing what he was asked seemed like the better option.

Later in the day, Benji set a timer on his phone to remind him when Sheila and Randolph were scheduled to land. He wanted to be back in front of the computer and ready to react to whatever came up. Which gave him a few hours of free time. He went downtown and paid for a pastry and an espresso with the few bucks he had in his pocket. It was at a different coffee shop than the one he used to work at, different than the one Patricia seduced him at.

It was cloudy but not rainy outside, cool but not cold. Mothers pushed strollers with one, sometimes two babies tucked safely inside. An elderly man walked slowly, either as if not in a hurry to get where he was headed or no longer capable of it. A middle-aged lady carried a small dog and talked into a wireless headphone that was oversized and looked ridiculous. One couple held hands and smiled, while another walked close to one another without touching, the woman with a scowl on her face.

Benji missed Justice.

*Justice.*

When he felt lost, he thought of her, of the night they spent on the beach, tangled in one another's bodies. Though unforgettable, it was not just the physical connection that made him desperate for more; it was also the undeniable emotional chemistry they shared. Justice was his new drug of choice, and he was having withdrawals. She made him higher than any joint ever could, no matter how potent it was.

Which was why waiting out Sheila and Randolph made Benji crazy. The longer they waited, the more time would pass before he would get to see Justice again. In his mind, he was still working on how he might get back to Fiji, both logistically and financially. He would come up with something, but he knew there was business to take care of first. His biggest fear was that Justice might forget about their evening together and about him in general.

Just like his father.

Were daddy issues a problem for men too? Cliché, Benji wondered, but so true. The day when his father brought him and his brothers to school, hugged them all, then never came home again lingered in the back of Benji's mind. While he did not think about it often, there would be times when he could not sleep where his mind would wander and fall upon that singular moment in his childhood; the moment that changed everything. His mother was different after that day. From a respected nurse to a street whore and junkie, all because her husband left them— and her holding the bag, specifically. Benji would always wonder what happened to his father that day, and what he would do if he ever saw him again.

He checked his phone. He had another hour or more before the flight landed, depending on delays. He killed enough time taking in the outdoors and those who lived in a higher social class than he ever would. Time to head back.

Patricia was there, wearing a clean outfit and a fresh batch of makeup and with damp hair—and smelling damn good. Too good. It gave Benji shivers, the memories of their good times together flooding through him. As much as he tried to forget, he never would. The memories of what they had physically would be forever implanted in his highlight reel, for whenever the well went dry—even if he knew he had the restraint to never act on those impulses again.

On the table, Gary's laptop was open. His phone was next to it, attached via cord to the USB port to charge. Benji's phone said fifty-five minutes left.

"What's up?" Benji said when he felt them both awkwardly staring at him. He wiped his face and checked his hand to see if snack remnants were there. Not the case.

"Where have you been?" Gary asked.

"Went for a walk. That's allowed, isn't it?"

"Of course."

"Then what's the problem?"

"I didn't say there was a problem."

"Maybe not with your words, but your face tells me there's a problem."

"No problem."

"Good. Then we're done?"

Gary shrugged.

Benji sat in his chair and swiveled.

An hour and a half passed. Gary and Patricia stood over his shoulder, all six eyes laser-focused on the map on Benji's monitor. According to Gary's contact at the airport, Sheila's plane should have landed a half hour ago. Benji confirmed it had with a quick visit to the airline's website.

More waiting.

Then it happened. A red dot. Benji sat up in a hurry, so fast he felt dizzy for a few seconds. He sensed Gary's energy shift behind him. Tense. Across the room, Gary's laptop pinged with a new alert. Benji spun and watched him rush over to it, then click frantically.

"Another video," Gary said.

Benji and Patricia walked over to take a peek.

More CCTV footage, this time from Roman Tmetuchl International Airport in Palau, according to the tag on the feed. Gary clicked on the video as Benji did a quick calculation in his mind about what time it should be in Palau and if there could have been any funny business. Without fact-checking, it all seemed to check out. No surprises so far.

As the video played, Benji's heart rate quickened. On the screen was Sheila again, wearing the same outfit and carrying the same bag as she had in the previous footage from Hawaii. Right behind her was Randolph, this time walking like a human rather than running to the bathroom like his prostate often forced him to do. Maybe he took a leak before the plane landed this time. Learned his lesson. Benji tried to hide his smirk as he thought about Randolph and his constant need to pee.

"We're a go, guys," Gary said. "They've both passed through customs. No switching flights. They're on the island, confirmed."

"You're not just letting them walk out of there, are you?" Benji said. "Why not detain them right there, right now?"

"Not your call."

"I know it's not, but damn. What are you waiting for?"

"Trust me, Benjamin. I have my reasons."

Benji did not know how to respond to that. The logic made zero sense. "So, what then? We chase them all over the island like last time? How'd that work out in Fiji?"

"Have faith. I have a guy on the inside following them. Wherever they end up, we'll know about it. We'll go to them and end this once and for all."

"When do we leave?" Patricia said with more excitement in her voice than was normal for a situation like this.

Gary slammed his laptop shut and glanced at his watch. "Ninety minutes. A car will be here to pick us up in ten. Get your stuff together."

"What about my computer?" Benji said.

"Leave it," Gary said. "It'll be fine here. Bring the necessities only. We'll be in and out, then back home before you know it."

This was it. One step closer to getting answers about what had been going on, and one step closer to being with Justice again.

*Justice.*

*I'm coming for you, my love. We'll be together soon.*

# CHAPTER THIRTEEN

*Ten years ago.* Things between Sheila's parents and her started deteriorating when she was fifteen. It was more than just an emotional distance that formed; it was something far, far worse. Something more permanent.

In the springtime, Sheila's mornings were business as usual. Sometimes she would bathe and eat breakfast and head off to school like every other kid. Other times, her father would join her in the kitchen while she ate and stand in the doorframe, saying nothing. On those days, she knew to clear her afternoon schedule because she had a drop-off to make for her father.

The older she got, the more difficult the drop-offs became. When she was younger and more childlike, most of the men she met with saw her as that—a child. But as she grew into a somewhat developed, sometimes beautiful, always innocent-looking teenager and young woman, she noticed men looked at her differently. Sometimes it was as simple as a double-take or squinted eyes or a menacing smile. Other, less controlled men would lick their lips or make a disgusting sucking noise with their tongue or even slowly caress her arm with the side of their finger.

Once, a man offered her all the cash in his pocket for her to give him something called a blowy. At the time, she was not sure what that meant, but judging by the look in his eyes—which she later identified as eroticism—it was not something she thought she wanted to partake in. Despite politely declining, the man continued to pressure her to the point where she felt unsafe. He pinned her back against the wall and towered over her, the smell of tobacco and liquor on his breath, and told her he was not asking anymore; she would do what he wanted, and she would like it.

Thankfully, another man entered the room and began hollering at the creep in Finnish, which gave Sheila a small window to slip under his arm and run out of the cigar shop. When she arrived home, her father was waiting for her as usual. She explained what happened and gave him the reason why the drop-off was not made. Instead of him comforting her and apologizing for the experience, he became angry—very angry.

And not with the man.

He became angry with her.

He blamed her for not zipping up her coat all the way and for wearing a blouse that exposed too much skin. They argued for a long while about it that night, Sheila and her father, and she went to bed feeling sad and defeated. While she lay awake in bed, her face wet with tears, she listened to her parents through the grate.

What she heard made her feel even worse.

"If she wants to act like a whore, then I'm going to treat her like one," her father said with anger still in his voice.

"She's fifteen," her mother said back, but not in a confrontational way, just as a matter of fact.

"Fifteen's the age for consent. Besides, do you know how much money we could make? These guys would go crazy for this. Fifteen is prime meat for them."

"I don't know. She's our daughter."

"Hell with that! Every girl is someone's daughter. Think about it, Pihla. We could branch out and grow the business. Drugs and sex go hand in hand. Once the word gets out, we'll be huge. Huge!"

"It's dangerous, Hector."

"Don't worry about that. I haven't been caught yet, have I? In how many years? Right?"

"Well, yes, that's true."

"See! I just need some time to figure out the details."

Sheila heard her parents kiss.

"This is going to be great," her father said with excitement in his voice. "I can't believe I didn't think about this until now. Today was a big day. Now that it's settled, I need to go make a phone call. I need to apologize to Lars about what happened today. He'll be thrilled to hear the news."

Her father's voice faded. A few seconds later, Sheila heard his office door open then close. A few seconds after that, she heard water running, which meant her mother was elbow deep in dirty dishes. As if the conversation she just had did not happen.

As if not bothered by the idea of her husband pimping out his fifteen-year-old daughter for sex.

Sheila's stomach roiled. While she did not know what the word the man—whose name she now knew was Lars—used earlier meant, she knew what sex was. She had not had it before, but she knew the basics from the class she took the year before in school. The thought of it, especially with someone like Lars, disgusted her.

What was worse was the next thought that crossed her mind.

*Minka.*

What about baby Minka? She was still a little kid, but how long would it be before their father had similar thoughts about her?

The thought made her sick.

She swallowed a bunch of times in a row to keep the bile down.

Once she recovered and the nausea passed, she slid out of bed and walked toward her shelf. On the top was a notepad with an attached pen, which she grabbed and brought back to her bed. Her eyes had adjusted to the darkness, so she could see exactly what she was doing. She began writing notes on the lines, reminders of things to consider.

It would take a lot of planning, she knew, and she would need some time to figure out all the details. But she also knew she had no choice in the matter. It was either put the work in or become her father's slave; be rented out like someone might rent a truck or a moving van.

She would not have it.

It was her life, and she would be in control of it. She was old enough, and smart enough, to get on by herself. All the drop-offs she did for her father had prepared her for how to deal with bad men, so she would manage just fine. She would use what she learned to get away from the bad men—and also her father, who, she now knew, was one of them. She would use all the information she had to escape, to save herself, before it was too late.

# CHAPTER FOURTEEN

*Present day.* Was it morning or afternoon? Randolph could not tell. He had been through this before in Fiji, and what he learned was that there was no getting used to it. So instead of worrying about it, he pulled the pin on his watch. Time did not matter.

One problem solved.

The next problem was not really much of a problem at all, turned out. Sheila had successfully made contact when they arrived yesterday, which meant the ball was rolling.

That was fast.

Way faster than Randolph expected.

*Okay, so what now?*

"Okay, so what now?" he asked Sheila over breakfast.

They were in a small café downtown sitting at an even smaller table. People bustled around them. Loud voices. The whirring of espresso machines and the cash register dinging and teenage girls yelling out order numbers buzzed.

"Well," Sheila said between bites of a croissant, "the logistics have been set up, so it's just a matter of getting from point A to point B. Which shouldn't be a problem. We've discussed this so many times, for so long."

"How do you feel about everything?"

"Relieved, mostly, though I realize we're not to the finish line yet. There are so many things that could go wrong, but I've planned for just about everything, so I'm feeling good. Really, really good." She smiled at him. "I'm glad you're here."

"I'm glad too."

"Are you?"

"Why wouldn't I be?"

"It's just, I don't know, a lot."

"Won't argue with you there. It is a lot. I know that. But I made my decision. And I think it was the right one."

"What made you come?"

"Honestly? You."

Sheila straightened. "Me?"

"You look surprised."

"I am surprised. After everything that happened. Just so you know, I never meant to—"

"I know."

"I just—"

"I know. I get it, I really do. And I understand. And I forgive you. Knowing what I know now, I would have done the same thing."

Tears welled in Sheila's eyes.

"I've thought so much about this, about everything you've told me, and I want to help you," he said. "Which is why I'm here. Not because of me, but because of you."

Sheila leaned forward and grabbed his hand over the table. Tears trickled down her cheeks. "Thank you."

They shared a moment just looking at one another. Even through her tears, she twinkled. Her eyes glistened. Her smile said more than words ever could. For all Randolph knew, which was a lot, she had not felt wanted in a very, very long time.

He knew the feeling.

Randolph leaned forward, rose his free hand, and wiped away the tears from Sheila's cheek with his thumb. The water soaked his fingertip. "Sheila, I—"

The next thing he knew, Sheila's lips were pressed against his, and his eyes were closed. The softness of her lips massaged his in a way he could not describe. A chill ran through his body, sending an electric jolt rushing from head to toe and back again. When she finally pulled away, he felt weak.

"We've got twenty-four hours to kill," Sheila said with lust in her eyes, "give or take."

"That's a long time."

"Yes, it is."

"What should we do?"

"I've got some ideas, if you're up for them."

He studied her. It was a look he was familiar with, from back in the day. Some things a man never forgets, and this was one of them. His body was ready—his whole body. "I'll pay the check."

•   •   •   •   •

Later—after, well, after—they lay awake next to one another, unclothed with their legs twisted together like a human-sized pretzel. Randolph felt a dull pressure in his prostate, but he also felt lighter, more relaxed. That made twice he had a full release in who knew how long, and both times had been with Sheila.

*Sheila.*

"Can I ask you something?" he said.

She turned and faced him, dropped her cheek on the feathery pillow.

"What happened in Fiji?" he asked.

"Which part?"

"All of it. I don't understand what happened."

"I take it you found the condo?"

"Of course. If you want to call it that."

The condo. Before Sheila left the States the first time, after the escape from Gary in Utah, it was discovered that she and Patricia had put a down payment on a condo in Fiji. Or, more accurately, Patricia put a down payment on a condo in Fiji with Randolph's money without his knowledge. He later learned that Sheila and Patricia—his then wife—were lovers who planned to start a new life together in that condo in Fiji after Randolph's death.

Which, of course, did not work out. Luckily for him.

It turned out, the whole plan was fabricated. Sheila had acted like she was into Patricia and planned to run away together, when in fact her plan all along had been to leave Patricia behind.

This was the part Randolph had been struggling with. Why would Sheila do that? What was her motivation?

"It was all for show," Sheila said. "The condo, I mean."

"How so?"

"I didn't have enough cash, so I needed to find someone who did, someone who could go fifty-fifty on it with me. Or more. Then I met Cheyenne—or Patricia, I guess—and I saw my way out. I've apologized a hundred times, and I'll apologize a hundred more if it would change what I did, but I know it can't. If I ever would have known that—"

"It's okay, Sheila. We don't have to rehash the past. I understand why you did it."

She sighed. "I know, but—"

"No buts. We're moving forward, not back."

"I know, you're right. You're right. So, anyway, you know what happened next. After Gary showed up at your son's house, I had no choice but to run. I could have used an alias to fly to Fiji, but I didn't. It was intentional. I knew if I used my real name, Gary would find out. And I also knew he'd find out about the condo and put two and two together. The name I used on the paperwork was a name Gary would know. Sure enough, he did."

"So, what, it was a trap?"

"Exactly. I knew he'd go to Fiji and look for me. I knew he'd spend time looking for the condo too. That's exactly what happened, and it gave me more time. As soon as I landed, I booked another flight out, back to the United States. Only this time, I used one of my other identities—a new one, one I'd never used before so Gary couldn't track me. And that was that."

Randolph lay there, just staring at her. Processing. That explained why the condo he and Benji found was so dilapidated, so unlived in—because it was. Sheila had not lived there, and had not planned to ever live there. It was all just for show.

He should have been angry. They really had been looking for a needle in a haystack, except there was no needle. No matter how long they stayed, how close they thought they were to finding her, they never would have found Sheila. Not ever. Not in Fiji. For that, Gary was right. Which made sense now, why Gary was so adamant about leaving; he must have figured it out and realized he had been duped.

Again.

Randolph broke out in laughter.

He laughed from the bottom of his belly, somewhere from deep inside his lungs. He laughed so hard he could not breathe. He laughed so hard he cried. He laughed so hard he almost peed—he had his prostate to thank for that.

"You're a genius," Randolph said after he finally composed himself. "A real genius. You know that?"

Sheila was smiling now, whether from the laugher contagion or out of relief. "I wouldn't say that. I'd call it more of being resourceful. Or desperate. Whatever it took."

"I get it. And I respect it. I respect you."

"Between Gary and the guys working for my dad, it's taken all I've had to stay out of their grasp all these years."

Randolph had feelings. Lots of them. "You're amazing."

Sheila smiled again and slid closer to him. He felt the warmth of her breath on his face.

"But I don't want to think about those other guys right now," she whispered. "The only man I want to think about right now is you."

Randolph leaned in and kissed her.

Then he wondered if he had it in him for round two.

Only one way to find out.

Only one way to find out.

# CHAPTER FIFTEEN

*Present day.* Many, many long, dull, boring hours later—after a forgettable in-flight meal, six tiny bags of pretzels, a handful of bathroom-sized cups of room temperature water, two and a half films, four magazines, and two trips to the toilet—they were in Palau. Benji, Gary, and Patricia. A trio of misfits with an unorthodox relationship and even stranger agenda.

Unlike last time, when Gary had given Benji and Randolph folders with more information than Benji could ever remember about Sheila, Benji had nothing to go on. What his role even was remained unclear. He could have asked, but he could not have been bothered. The more he knew, the less he understood. So in this case, *naivety* was good. He was simply tagging along until requested to do something.

Gary paid for three rooms in a rinky-dink motel-style place near the water. Benji sat on the bed inside his room and was overcome with the feeling of being bushed. Since he did not ask what he was supposed to do, he had nothing on the agenda, as far as he know. So he sprawled out on the bed, kicked off his shoes, and napped. It had been more than a couple of days.

When he awoke later, he felt better. Groggy and hungry, a bit lovesick, but nothing he could not handle. With a little nourishment and maybe a cold beer, he would be ready for whatever Gary wanted him to do.

But that would have to wait.

His phone buzzed with a new message.

It was from Gary.

Benji read it and immediately felt more awake, semi-alert, ready to spring into action. He headed outside and closed the door behind him. Gary and Patricia were waiting for him in the parking lot.

"I got your message," Benji said as he approached.

"I see that," Gary said.

"What's up?"

Gary looked at Patricia then back to Benji. He had a smile on his face. "We got them."

"Meaning?"

"I've got my guy on them. I know right where they are. And it's definitely them. Confirmed."

Now Benji's heart was really pumping. He could not believe this was actually happening. It seemed like they had been chasing forever. And now, they would finally catch them. Her. Sheila.

But Randolph too.

"Time to put your game face on, Benjamin. You ready?"

That was the question. Was he ready? Would he have it in him to go through with this? Sheila was one thing—he could not have cared less about what happened to her, not after the scheme she put him through. But Randolph was different. They had gotten close in Fiji. Father-son-like. Would he have what it took to take him down to save himself?

Benji felt Gary and Patricia both piercing him with their stares. Patricia was cold and had been out to get Randolph from the start. Gary had been after Sheila for a while and had proven not to care about anyone but himself; collateral damage was never something he considered. This would be easy for both of them. No skin off their backs. None whatsoever. For Benji, it would not be so easy, and they knew that. And they knew he knew they knew that.

"What's it going to be?" Gary asked.

Like Benji really had a choice.

"I'm here, aren't I?"

Gary almost smiled. Almost. "Well good, because the cab's going to be here in"—Gary pulled out his phone and peeked at the screen, then looked past Benji, somewhere over his shoulder—"now."

Benji turned and saw a cab slowly rolling in.

"Let's go," Gary said. "Let's go end this shit."

# CHAPTER SIXTEEN

*Ten years ago.* As the school year wound down, Sheila's grades slipped. She knew it, though her parents did not. She had been accustomed to earning As and Bs throughout her life, so it was a surprise to her teachers when they started seeing Cs and Ds and Es, even one F for an assignment she chose not to complete. Her teachers asked her to stay after class so they could talk, all of whom asked her the same set of questions. What was going on? Was she okay? Was there something happening at home? Sheila learned to smile and giggle and make light of the situation to ease her teachers' worries.

She felt bad for blaming Minka—she was being fussy lately, or she was teething and not sleeping much, Sheila told them— but her teachers bought it. They understood. Some gave her time to make up the assignments or allowed her to turn them in late for partial credit. What Minka would not know would not hurt her, right? She was just a toddler. No harm, no foul. Whatever it took to get her teachers off her back—and most importantly, for them not to call her parents about it—Sheila had to do.

The real reason her grades started slipping was because she spent as much of her free time as possible preparing her escape. Everything else was secondary. That included homework.

While deep in her preparations, she knew she had to keep up the façade of business as usual so to avoid raising any suspicions from her parents. Her father had not mentioned anything about sex to her, and she had not overhead any other conversions about it between her parents, but she noticed her father working more. He left his office only to eat and use the bathroom; aside from that, he was locked inside whenever Sheila was home. She never even saw him sleep. All of which told her he too was deep into researching and preparing his next plan—to offer her body to his business associates in exchange for a few extra kronor in his pocket.

He was the driving force behind her focus.

She kept the notepad with her thoughts under her mattress and was sure to make her bed every day so her mother would not find it. She even pushed it toward the center instead of the edge, just to be careful. She could not get busted on this. If she did, it would be over just as quickly as it started—and never executed.

As usual, she would make occasional drop-offs for her father after school some days. She noticed the men looked at her differently, as if they knew they just had to wait a while longer and they would be given her father's permission to use her body.

She took advantage of that.

As much as she could coordinate her plan on paper, the one missing element to being able to carry it out was money. She was only fifteen and had never held a job, so the only money she had was what she saved from birthdays or coins she found on the street. Taking money from her mother's purse, even small amounts, felt wrong. And too risky. She had to be careful.

But she also needed a lot of cash, and a lot of cash fast. And she knew the men her father associated with had money because they put some in her backpack in exchange for whatever her father was trading it for. She thought back to what her father had said to her the night she came home after that uncomfortable confrontation with the man named Lars. She remembered her father blaming her for not zipping up her coat and for showing too much skin.

Which gave her an idea.

To make money, she had to spend some money, so that was what she did. After school one afternoon, she hopped on the bus and took it to the clothes market with all the money she had stashed away. She perused through the shelves and racks looking for the styles of shirts her father had described, and eventually, she found some.

She studied herself in the mirror in the changing room. For the first time, she really looked at herself. She thought she was prettiest when her hair was down and free-flowing and when she wore just a touch of makeup around her eyes. When she turned and looked at herself from the side, she saw what her father did—her chest was growing. She had worn a bra for a few years, but all the ones she had felt tight.

The shirts her size fit her well, as they should have. But fitting well also meant she could not see her humps as much in the mirror, so she tried one size smaller. When she pulled the smaller-sized shirt over her head, her chest stretched the material quite a lot. It stretched so much, the bottom was not long enough to cover her belly. Her waist was thin, though, so she looked good. More than good—dare she say, hot.

It was perfect.

She kept the new shirts hidden from her mother. She wore them under her regular shirts on the days she made drop-offs for her father. Before she left school those days, she took off the top layer so only the new, smaller, tighter shirt was left. Then she made the drop-offs.

When she saw the looks on the men's faces—wide eyes, mouths agape—she finally understood what her father had been talking about. The men she met with would stare at her chest, where the V-neck exposed cleavage, instead of in her eyes. Some would slur their words instead of speaking in coherent sentences. Then one time, she tried something. Her heart was beating so hard and so fast, she was afraid the man might see the fear and try to take advantage of her. But she did it anyway, because if someone was going to benefit from her body, she thought it might as well be her.

"Want to see them?" she said to the man, who looked back at her with a childlike smile that she found both flattering and completely embarrassing for a grown man.

"Hell yes," he said.

"Five hundred krona."

The man did not hesitate. He reached behind his back and returned with a leather wallet. Five seconds later, Sheila had five hundred krona in her hand, which was equivalent to almost fifty United States dollars. She lifted her shirt and held the position for a few seconds. After, she warned him not to tell her father, to which he immediately agreed and promised he would not. Drool practically fell from his lips.

That was how it started. At first, it was just lifting her shirt up. As she got braver and more confident, she began pulling her bra down too—for five hundred more krona, of course. Some men were willing to go further than that, and give her more money. Some would give her five hundred more if she let them touch them. One man was so desperate, she kept rejecting him until he left the room and came back with more than ten thousand krona in cash—or about one thousand United States dollars. She almost felt bad for him, for how pathetic he was about it, but she pocketed the cash and looked away while he squeezed her chest for a few seconds.

Once she learned this, about how far men would go just to look at or touch her chest, she began charging more. A lot more. By the end of the summer, she had enough money saved inside a hollowed-out book she kept under her bed that it would not even shut anymore. At that point, she thought she had earned as much money as she could before it was too late—before her father somehow found out.

One September morning, three days after she turned sixteen, she packed her school bag as usual. She ate breakfast. She brushed her teeth. She said goodbye to her parents. Before she left, she acted as if she forget something upstairs, which was not untrue. She dropped to her knees and reached under the bed, pulled out the hallowed out book. She folded all the money that was inside and slipped it into her bra. Then she lifted the mattress, pulled out her notepad, and slipped that into her backpack in between her books. Before leaving her bedroom, she tucked the sheet under the mattress, smoothed the top, and zipped her backpack.

Downstairs, she wrapped Minka up in her arms and hugged her tight. They pulled apart and made eye contact, and Sheila used all her strength not to cry. It would be a while before she saw Minka again, she knew, but she would never forget about her. She would come back for her one day, somehow, someway. Sometime before their father deemed her to be old enough for his associates. Sometime before she was fifteen.

Sheila hugged her mom again and told her goodbye. Her father was already gone, his office door closed. Then Sheila hooked her thumbs around the straps of her backpack and walked outside into the sun.

She went to school like she was supposed to. Her teacher took attendance in the morning like every other day. Sheila waited twenty minutes before asking to go to the bathroom. But instead of going to the bathroom, she walked down the hallway toward her locker. Inside was her backpack with the clothes she packed the night before, the extra toiletries from the closet she guessed her mother would not notice to be missing, and her notepad. She left her books behind, grabbed the bag, tossed it over her shoulder, and walked out the backdoor without anyone noticing her.

That was the last day she ever went to school.

Instead of taking a right and heading home, Sheila took a left and walked to the bus station. She bought a single bus ticket. Nobody looked twice or asked why she was not in school or showed any sense of caring in the least. Which was precisely what she hoped would happen. Twenty minutes later, she boarded the bus and left, leaving Lund, Sweden, in the rearview, never to return again.

And she never did. Never.

# CHAPTER SEVENTEEN

*Present day.* The next day came faster than Randolph thought he deserved. Typical life: time flew when you did not want it to, and it dragged when you desperately wanted it to go faster. Sometime during daylight hours, Sheila received a message on her phone, and her face lit up. Without saying anything, Randolph knew what that meant.

It was on.

He and Sheila got ready. She phoned for a cab. They waited downstairs until it arrived. When it did, they hopped in the back and Sheila gave the driver the location of the meeting spot. The ride was silent aside from the humming of the rubber against the gravel underneath.

They arrived. Sheila paid the driver and thanked him, and she and Randolph got out. The cab drove off, leaving them alone with their backs to what gave off the vibe of being an abandoned warehouse. No sign. Boarded up windows. Graffiti bubble letters covered the wall that faced the street. A cracked plastic cup and an empty fast food bag littered the ground. The air smelled salty, but with a hint of garbage.

They stood. They waited.

Then they stood some more, and they waited some more. A lot of time seemed to have passed.

"Are we in the right place?" Randolph asked Sheila when the waiting became unbearable. He immediately regretted it.

Sheila coldly disregarded his question.

More time passed.

Randolph had other similar questions, but he kept them to himself; Sheila knew what she was doing. He glanced at her and saw the angst in the way she stood—an anxious heel tapping, fidgety fingers, her body in constant motion—and he felt the energy shift.

And not in a good way.

"It shouldn't be taking this long," Sheila admitted. "I don't like this."

Randolph did not know how to respond, so he said nothing. He just stood there and shoved his hands in his pockets. A light sea breeze kissed his skin and sent a chill through his core. His gaze fell upon what began as a tiny speck on the horizon, a nothing. Meaningless. But as nothing but stillness happened around them, the speck grew larger, closer, though still unclear from his vantage point. He kept watching.

Eventually the speck grew so large that it was unmistakably coming toward them, though Randolph could not make out what it was. He pointed at it. "See that?"

"Been watching it."

"And?"

"Ask me again in two minutes."

Randolph's heart raced.

After more than a minute but definitely less than two, he said, "What about now?"

"Something's not right."

"What do we do?"

"Just wait."

They did.

The speck came into view. A white sedan. Ordinary. Nothing flashy about it. The only aspect of it that looked a little off was how the windows were blacked out. Which meant Randolph could not see inside, even after the sedan pulled up in front of them and stopped.

"Stay cool," Sheila said to him with a slight tremble in her voice, although she seemed anything but at this point.

Randolph was tense, his fingers loosely clutched into fists dangling at his sides, no longer in his pockets.

Exhaust smoke faded from the tailpipe. The brake lights dimmed. Then the driver's side door opened and an average-looking light-skinned man appeared—average height, average length of haircut, average weight. He closed the door and walked around the car without so much as looking at them. Randolph's fists were no longer loose.

"Sheila Backe," the man said as a statement, not a question.

"Yes?"

Then: "Randolph Spiers."

"Uh, yeah?"

"Good," the man said. He pulled out his phone and pressed a button. A couple of seconds later, he said into the phone, "I've got them."

Then he hung up.

"Who are you?" Sheila asked him.

"Come with me."

"We're not going anywhere," Sheila said.

"Oh, is that so?" The man smiled, but not in a friendly way. Then he reached behind his back and swung his arm forward again. This time, with a pistol in his hand—and it was pointed directly at Sheila's face. "How about now?"

•　　•　　•　　•　　•

Their hands and wrists were bound behind their backs. Randolph could not say how Sheila was handling it, but he was not handling it well. Not at all. It was not only the angle at which his elbows were bent, painfully stretching his tendons beyond comfort, but also the sharp ache in his lower back from having his arms at that angle. Anxious perspiration soaked his shirt from underneath. His armpits felt sticky.

Where they were, he could not say for sure. After they were bound with zip ties and shoved into the back of the sedan, Randolph mostly conked out mentally. Instead of watching where they were being taken—they, surprisingly, were not blindfolded—Randolph found himself trying to focus on deep breathing and relieving the pressure on his joints. He had kept himself together, but he was teetering. He felt on edge, close to losing it. When it came to fight or flight, he was option three.

Panic.

Despite all that, he composed himself just enough to get to his feet when the sedan stopped and the door opened, and to follow the man with the gun into the building.

Randolph stood alone. Just him and a concrete floor with a water stain in the corner and bright overhead lighting. An industrial garage, maybe? Or it could have been a giant incinerator that was about to boil him to a crisp.

Okay, even he admitted that might have been a bit dramatic.

But could he say for sure that it was not?

After a minute or two, the door on the far end of the open room opened, and in walked Sheila with the man behind her—presumably with the gun pressed against the small of her back, just like it had been with Randolph. Sheila walked toward him with her head pointing downward in defeat. Her steps were short and tight as if her ankles were chained together, her pace childlike.

The man shoved her from behind, nearly sending her tumbling forward. Randolph instinctively lurched forward as if to catch her, only to remember that his hands were bound behind him. He was completely helpless. And defenseless. And, in what seemed all but certain, fucked.

"Don't do anything stupid," the man said. "I'll be back."

Neither Randolph nor Sheila said anything.

He watched the man's back as he walked away, opened the door, and slipped outside. Then he heard a lock engage.

Sheila fell to the concrete almost immediately and began wailing. "Stupid, stupid, stupid! I feel so stupid!"

"Come on now, you're not stupid."

"I should have known. Everything was going so smoothly. It was too easy. Too damn easy!"

Randolph did not know what to say. She was right. Everything had been seamless. And as Randolph had learned, things were never easy with Sheila.

*Sheila.*

"I'm sorry," he said.

She looked up at him. "Sorry for what?"

"Sorry about all this. I'm sorry it's happening."

She sighed. "It's not your fault."

"It's not yours either."

"No, but—"

"You did everything right. You did the best you could. We're not giving up."

"Thank you for trying to make me feel better, but it doesn't change the fact that we're both zip-tied behind our backs and locked in this room with no way out."

True.

Randolph crouched down and grunted, and joined Sheila on the cold concrete. He shimmied on his backside until his back was pressed against the equally cold wall.

"How are we going to get out of here?" Sheila asked him. Her eyes begged him like a helpless puppy's might.

"Do you have anything on you that could cut through these things?" he asked.

"Like what?"

"Anything sharp. Anything at all."

She did not respond right away, as if thinking. "All I have is some cash. Everything else is back in the room."

"Yeah, me too."

"So what do we do now?"

Randolph shook his head. He did not know. He let his shoulders sink.

It did not take long for the energy to shift again. Outside the door, it sounded like someone was fidgeting with the lock. Randolph tensed and pressed his back harder against the wall, as if he might be able to push it over and escape. But instead of a sprint to safety, the door popped open. The man with the pistol was back, only this time, it was not the same man—and he had company.

Sheila was the first to speak: "Oh, shit."

# CHAPTER EIGHTEEN

*Present day.* Benji rode in the back of the cab with Patricia, to his misery. Even with a seat between them, her proximity to his body revolted him. It was amazing to him how far they had come in such a short time—from passionately physical lovers to anything but—but it was what it was. Now that he knew her deal, who she really was, he no longer wanted anything to do with her. Thankfully, she kept her distance from him, not even looking in his direction. It was as if she had finally gotten the message and learned that Benji wanted her gone.

If only he could have been that lucky.

In the front, Gary sat with the driver and gave him instructions on where they were headed. None of it meant anything to Benji. Frankly, he did not really want to know; he would have preferred to avoid this situation altogether, but it did not look like that was going to happen. His stomach knotted at the thought of what Gary might ask him to do. He was still unconvinced he could go through with it, whatever it was, even though he had the feeling his life as he knew it was at stake.

*Justice.*

That was his motivation; she was his motivation. But he was worried it would not be enough.

The cab pulled up outside an old brick building and stopped. Gary held his phone up and glanced between the screen and the building. Benji leaned forward to get a peek but could not see anything.

"Is this the right place?" Gary asked the driver.

"If your address is right, then yes."

"Hang on one second." Gary typed a message into his phone and waited. After a few seconds, he said, "Okay, confirmed. Back side of the building."

"Want me to drop you off?"

"No. Absolutely not. Take this"—Gary handed the driver a wad of cash—"and pretend this never happened. You never saw us, and you've never been here before. Got it?"

Benji's stomach roiled.

"Geez, thanks, dude. I'll do pretty much whatever you want for this kind of dough."

"Good. Now, be gone." Gary turned and faced Benji and Patricia. "Let's go."

They all opened their respective doors and stepped out. The cab sped away. Benji watched it fade into the horizon, and he knew he was in for a world of trouble. Just a sense he had, a feeling. A sixth sense. Without giving himself away, he quickly scanned his surroundings. They seemed to be in a neglected part of town with all its dilapidated buildings, a flipped trash receptacle, and a haze that smelled of the unliving. There were no signs of a vehicle, no tire tracks beyond the one the cab just left. Not a sound to be heard. Somewhere in the not so distant distance, a line of trees offered some semblance of life.

Benji felt a rush of fear, sending a shockwave through his body. Bumps pushed their way out from underneath his skin and covered his forearms. He quickly massaged them back down with his opposite hand before anyone could notice—he could not show how he felt; only the weak showed fear.

"What is this shit hole?" Patricia said.

At least that was something Benji could agree with her on.

"Follow me," Gary said as he began walking. "We're going around the back."

Patricia obliged, and so did Benji. He lingered in the back, ready to make a run for it if he found his chance. By the looks of it, there was nowhere to run to, and certainly nowhere to hide, so that seemed all but a pipe dream. The line of trees looked about a million miles away and unattainable. Benji was left with no choice but to play along and do what he was told.

For now.

He felt focused and entirely aware of everything around him, his senses heightened. Sharp. His batteries were recharging and ready to be put on full blast if needed. He would keep himself under control until then, if the right time presented itself.

The back side of the building was not much different than the front. The visuals were the same, the misery just as apparent. The only difference was a single gray door near the end of the building. It was unnumbered. Benji did not want to know what was on the other side, though he had a guess.

Outside the door stood a man smoking a cigarette, a cloud of smoke enveloping his face like a mask. One of his legs was up, the foot pressed against the brick behind him next to the door for support. Benji could not make out any features from the distance between them.

"Stay here," Gary said. "Let me go talk to this guy."

Benji stopped once Patricia did. They kept their distance and watched.

Gary approached the man and shook his hand. The two men appeared to engage in a normal conversation for a short time. The man with the cigarette pointed behind his back and blew a massive puff of smoke above his head.

What happened next was unexpected.

As if shot from a cannon, Gary's right arm sprung forward and grabbed the other man by the hair. Then his arm catapulted the other man's head forward and directly against the brick. The man fell like a stone in an instant, flattened against the pavement, unmoving.

Benji felt his eyes pop open. At first, he was not sure he saw what he thought he saw. He could not have; things like that did not happen in real life. But then Gary bent down and searched the man on the ground, rolling him from side to side as if he were a doll. At that point, reality hit Benji, and he knew he was in serious trouble.

Before he even had time to think, Gary was up and walking toward them, a gun dangling in his hand. Benji snuck a glance at Patricia to gauge her reaction. Her arms were crossed and she shook her head in obvious anger or disappointment. Or both. Coming from her, it was significant.

"What the hell was that?" she asked Gary when he was in earshot.

"Don't talk," he said in return.

"Seriously, what the hell was that?"

"I said"—the gun rose in Gary's hand—"don't talk."

Patricia gasped.

Benji felt his shoulders sink.

"Both of you," Gary said, "come with me. In there."

Benji knew what he meant without him having to explain it. They would walk through that gray door and into whatever was on the other side, where they would more likely than not be killed or left there to die. And considering where they were, it seemed unlikely that their bodies would ever be found.

This time, Gary pushed Benji and Patricia in front of him and walked behind them. "Walk," he said.

Benji did what he was told. He felt humiliated. He suspected he was being played the entire time, yet he had no proof. Now he did, but it was too late to do anything about it. Gary had a gun, Benji did not. For all he knew, Gary might pull the trigger at any second and end it all right now. He could not put it past Gary to shoot him in the back, just like a coward would.

Benji had read somewhere that your life flashes before you when you are about to die. He was not sure if it had to do with passing through to the other side or if it was a psychological phenomenon that manifested itself through a near-death experience. Either way, it did not happen to him. He did not see his childhood flash before him—not his mother as a nurse or his mother as a whore; not his father as a working man or his father as a weak mean who abandoned his family; not his brothers as kids or as they were living their lives today, completely isolated from Benji. He saw nothing.

It could have been because his life was meaningless and loveless, and therefore his psyche had nothing worthy of flashing; no memories worth remembering. Or it could have been because he was unworthy of passing over and therefore was not given the privilege of being reminded of happier moments one last time.

Or, just maybe, it was not his time yet.

He stopped before he got to the door. He looked down at the man on the gravel. Blood poured out from a split in his forehead and pooled around him. A still lit cigarette burned next to him on the ground. He looked dead, but Benji had no way of knowing. For all he knew, the man was just knocked out cold and bleeding profusely. At the rate the blood poured out, it did not look good for him, even if he was still technically alive.

Gary walked around Benji and fumbled with some keys—presumably one of the items he found when he searched the maybe dead, maybe not dead yet body on the ground. When he found what he was looking for, he slipped the key into the keyhole on the gray door and disengaged the lock. He pulled the door open and ushered Benji and Patricia inside.

Benji looked across the big, empty room and even though he should not have been surprised, he still was. It almost seemed too hard to believe.

"Well, well, well," Gary said. "Look what the cat dragged in? Isn't this about to be the family reunion from hell?"

# CHAPTER NINETEEN

*Ten years ago.* The day Sheila walked out of school and hopped a bus out of town was the first day of the rest of her life. She knew things would be different for her. Where would she sleep? What would she eat? Where would she go? Most importantly, how would she stay hidden?

Thankfully, she had answers to all those questions already mapped out in her notepad. Plus, she had quite a lot of money and the resources to get more now that she knew how much men desired her body. When she wore makeup, she thought she looked older than she was. Sixteen was close to eighteen anyway, so she felt confident that she could pretend she was a couple of years older if she needed to be. That was the biggest concern. She packed a lot of makeup.

The bus brought her directly to the seaport in Lomma, Sweden. The harbor was filled with sailboats of all sizes and shapes, and even a few boats without sails. Groups of fishermen carried tackle boxes and long rods and smoked cigars. She saw more than a few sailor hats. Some adults looked at her with curious eyes as she walked past them with a backpack over her shoulder, but most did not. An elderly woman whacked an elderly man on the shoulder and not so subtly pointed at her. Sheila put her head down and quickly walked in the opposite direction as the elderly man started walking toward her. Youth was on her side, so she could lose the curious man without much effort—and without bringing attention to herself by running. She weaved in and out of crowds, trying her best to stay in front of adults who were taller than her. The elderly man never caught up.

Getting onto one of the sailboats posed a challenge more difficult than she planned. She approached three men on their boats, all of whom appeared to be the captain. The first man she asked laughed her off the dock and said he would not get involved in such shenanigans as transporting an underage girl across the border. She argued she was not underage, but he did not buy it. He suggested she go back home where she belonged. She did not take his advice.

The second man she approached lowered his sunglasses and peered over the top, his eyes scanning her from head to toe. He asked her what she would give him in return if he let her on board. She recognized the look in his eye—it was awfully similar to the one Lars gave her that day—so she turned around and walked away just as quickly as she arrived.

When she got to the third man, desperation took over. Many of the sailboats had departed by now, and the crowd was thinning out on the docks. She feared she would stand out more than she wanted to if that happened. She tried a different approach.

"Excuse me, can you help me?" she said to the man. She made her voice sound like she was in trouble.

"Are you all right?" the man said to her in a tone that told her she might be in luck.

"Actually, there's a man. He's after me. He said he was going to take me and—"

"Which man?" The sailor looked concerned now. He took a step off his boat and onto the dock. He shielded his eyes and looked beyond her.

"I . . . I don't know where he went. I'm scared."

While the sailor was looking elsewhere for the invisible bad guy, Sheila stared at the sun for a few seconds until her eyes watered.

"Please," she said when the sailor looked back at her. "Please help me."

The man looked older than her father, but not as old as her grandfather. Wrinkles curled up on his forehead. Parts of his beard was gray, but not all of it. She thought he looked like someone who would not do anything to hurt her. If anything, he looked like he might do the opposite. She hoped her instincts were right.

"Where are you headed?" he asked.

"Copenhagen."

"Denmark?"

She nodded.

"Oh, dear," he said. "That's a long way. I won't be able to get you to Copenhagen, but—"

"As far as you can bring me. Please. I have money."

The man paused and looked at her, studied her. "How old are you?"

"Eighteen."

The man did not acknowledge that. Did that mean he did not believe her?

"I'm headed to Malmö," he said. "There's a train station there that could get you to Copenhagen."

"Thank you! Yes!" Sheila ran toward him and shook his hand in gratitude before he had the chance to change his mind. "How much?"

He held up his free hand. "Don't bother. Keep your money. Now hurry, come on board before he finds you."

And that was that.

Turned out, not all men were creeps. Some were sweet and protective like men were supposed to be. This man was one of them.

She later learned the sailor's name was Mikael and he had a daughter about her age, just a couple of years younger—which meant they were actually the same age, since he thought she was eighteen. She felt guilty for lying to the man, but she knew she had no choice. Good men like Mikael would never help her leave the region, never mind the country, but they would help if she was in trouble. Despite it being on false pretenses, she would never forget what Mikael did for her. Because without him, she never would have made it to Denmark.

· · · · · ·

The one thing Sheila always wondered was how long it took her parents to notice that she was missing. Her mother should have expected her right after school since there was no drop-off that day. What was the level of concern when Sheila did not show up after school? Did they call the police? The only reason her father would have cared would have been if it impacted his business, so maybe calling the police would have been too risky. Even if it was Sheila who was the one on the front lines doing all the dirty work. The police could have learned that if they started digging; it would not have taken much.

Sheila had never been to Copenhagen before. She thought it was beautiful. The people wandering around the city looked like her. There was nothing unordinary about the shops. What was different than back home, having lived inland, was the canals. Majestic waters shone under the night stars as Sheila strolled along the boardwalk, tiny ripples forming as fish leaped. The city housed some of the tallest buildings she had ever seen, plus unique architecture unlike anything at home. She spent much of the early evening casually taking it all in, feeling completely alive and independent and powerful.

None of the hotels would rent her a room since she was under eighteen, but that was okay. And expected. She spent a pleasant night under the stars on a bench in the town center, neither full of regret nor afraid. Luck fell her way as the temperature did not fall too low and the precipitation held out. The evening was truly magical.

As written in her notepad, the first order of business the following day was to find someone who could make her a fake ID that said she was indeed a legal adult; doing so would open up so many more possibilities for her, and would make her journey that much easier. The problem was, it was not as easy as asking the locals where someone could get one. That part took some figuring out.

Luckily, again, she was fully prepared. All the research had been done ahead of time, so all she had to do was go to the places she had written in her notepad and see who might be willing to give her one. Eventually she found someone, although it cost more of her money than she had planned, which set her back a little. It also took two full days longer than she had been led to believe, which meant she had to camp outdoors for longer than expected. It sprinkled for a short time on night two, but not enough to cause a hassle.

Once she had the ID in hand and found a motel that would accept cash, she locked herself in the room, discarded all her now disgusting clothes, and spent an hour in the shower. That night, she slept better than she had since before baby Minka was born, and she felt grateful for having gotten that far.

Grateful, but not satisfied.

As much as she grew to love Denmark, it was never her final destination. It was much too close to home. Her plan all along had been to get as far west as she could, as far west as was safe. She read America was considered the land of opportunities, which sounded nice. If she could find a way to get there, she thought she might have a chance to make something of herself—and to eventually have the means to rescue baby Minka.

The problem was, her research had only gotten her to a certain point, and America was not part of it. First things first: getting out of Europe.

# CHAPTER TWENTY

*Present day.* Randolph could not believe what his eyes showed him. The cast of characters before him—well, across the room from him—was not a group he could imagine being together in a million years. It was logistically not possible. Not here. The last time he saw her, she was locked up in Iowa where she belonged.

"Patricia?" he said, completely dumbfounded. He paid the others no mind. "What the hell are you doing here?"

"Wow," she said. "You sure know how to make a lady feel special. Nice to see you too."

"Why am I not surprised to see you two together?" Gary O'Reilly said to Randolph. He meant Randolph and Sheila.

Randolph ignored him.

"Seriously, Patricia," Randolph said to his ex-wife, "how are you here? Shouldn't you be back in Iowa?"

"Shouldn't you?"

"No, actually. I'm not the one charged with attempted murder."

She had no rebut to that.

"What is this?" Sheila said. "What's going on?"

"Benji?" Randolph said to Benji, having recovered from the shock of seeing Patricia outside of a prison. He was just as surprised to see him too, especially with Patricia.

Benji lifted his wrist in a wave, but said nothing. There was a look on his face Randolph had never seen before. He could not place it.

Then seemingly all at once, everyone spoke at the same time. All Randolph made out was a jumbled mess of words, none of which made a coherent sentence. Benji said something about Gary and a gun; Sheila said something to Gary about being an asshole; Patricia said something about a dead guy.

Hold on, what dead guy?

"What dead guy?" Randolph asked.

"The fucking guy outside!" Patricia said. "Bleeding to death outside the door."

Huh?

Everyone spoke over one another again.

That was until Gary stepped in. He lifted a gun over his head and pulled the trigger.

Randolph ducked and tried to cover his head, but his hands were still bound. His ears rang then buzzed as something snapped, then they popped as if underwater. His entire body jolted with pain.

The room was suddenly silent.

"Will you all shut up now?" Gary asked.

"Have you lost your mind?" Patricia said to him. Randolph recognized the anger in her voice, and on her expression; it was something he had seen on more than a couple of occasions over the years. "You could have shot somebody."

"That would have been tragic."

Patricia huffed as if taken aback by the insult.

Gary turned his attention to Sheila. A vicious smirk overtook his expression. "Sheila Backe," he said. "The one that got away one too many times. Looks like it's all finally caught up with you, hasn't it? No windows in this room, sweetheart. Don't think you're going to get out of this one."

"Leave her alone, Gary," Randolph said. He felt the blood constrict in his wrists as he clenched his fingers into fists. He wanted nothing more than to break free from the tie and give Gary the slug he deserved.

"Stop trying to be a hero," Gary shot back. "I think you've done enough already, don't you?"

"I have no idea what you're talking about."

Which was true. He did not.

"Yeah, yeah. Save it. Now"—Gary stepped toward Sheila, his thumb caressing the top of the gun—"I think we have some unfinished business here. You and me."

"I don't think so," Sheila said. She backed away from him as far as she could until her back was pressed against the wall. Her lips creased in defense, but Randolph saw the tremor in her knees; she was afraid.

Randolph watched helplessly. His instincts told him to lunge at Gary and attack him to protect Sheila, but his mind reminded him how stupid that would be. No hands versus two hands, one with a gun, was suicide. He had no choice but to stand there and watch.

Gary stepped closer and closer to Sheila, stopping only when there was nowhere else to go. He was so close, he could have stuck his tongue out and licked Sheila's face. Her face was twisted away from him, her neck flush against the wall.

"There's only one thing I like more than getting even," Gary whispered loud enough for the room to hear. "Do you know what that is?"

Shelia said nothing.

Randolph saw her chest rapidly rise and fall under Gary's shadow. It ate Randolph up to admit that he could do nothing to help her. He had to think of something, and fast.

"Being rich," Gary said. "Being filthy, stinking rich. And now that I finally have you, that's exactly what I'm going to be. We should celebrate." He eyed her up and down. "Want to celebrate with me? I have an idea of something we could do."

Randolph could not stand it any longer. Anger boiled in him like a raging inferno about to burst. "Gary! Leave her the fuck alone, you cocksucker!"

Gary turned and faced him. The outline of his jaw popped from underneath his skin. Randolph had struck a nerve. "What did you just say to me?"

Rage still burned hot. Adrenaline shot through Randolph's body. "I said stay the fuck away from her."

"After that." Gary began walking toward Randolph now.

"I called you a cocksucker." Randolph held his ground. If only his hands were free . . .

"Is that what you think I am?" Gary walked over and stood in front of Randolph now.

Randolph smelled the sweat on the man's neck. "That's what I said. Cocksucker."

At first, Gary did not react. He stood still and silent and just looked at Randolph, expressionless. Then a smirk broke through on his face, lifting his lip upward. Then he smiled through gritted teeth.

Randolph sensed what was going to happen before it actually did. Somewhere in his periphery, he caught a glimpse of Gary's finger slipping off the trigger of the gun and sliding onto the barrel. His fingers grabbed a hold and his arm swung above his head.

It happened so fast. Randolph saw it develop, but he did not have time to react to it. Instinctively, he leaned to the right as Gary's arm swung down and thrashed the butt of the gun against the side of Randolph's head.

Fire exploded through his skull. He felt woozy and weightless all at once. After the second time Gary hit him, Randolph's knees buckled. On the third, he went down. His world spun horizontally then disappeared as he hit the floor.

# CHAPTER TWENTY-ONE

*Present day.* Benji stood frozen with shock and he watched Randolph fall to the concrete and go limp. He was not sure which, but one of the women screamed. Gary stood over Randolph's body and breathed heavily, grunting as if he might shapeshift into a green monster.

Benji knew what he had to do. He was in danger and Randolph was in danger. And as much as he did not particularly care about what happened to Patricia or Sheila, for that matter, they were in danger too. If they did not do something, they would all die in this room.

He was not ready to die.

Benji gritted his teeth, clenched his hands, screamed his anger into reality, and ran toward Gary with the fury of an angry bull. He screamed louder with each step to the point where his throat burned and he was just about out of breath. There was not much space between them, so he covered it quickly. Just before he ran completely out of breath, he lunged forward, his arms outstretched, and crashed into Gary, who had partially turned and faced him.

Benji heard something solid smack against the floor but felt no pain. The impact dislodged Gary's weapon and it slid away. Benji saw it come to a stop next to him, close to being within an arm's length, but he let it go. His hands were tied up with one of Gary's limbs—he could not tell which.

They fought. Benji dropped an elbow against Gary's face and watched the blood pour out from his nose. Gary blindly swung a closed fist and landed the side of his hand against Benji's forehead. Benji jabbed his ribs with his strong arm, but not very hard; he had little room for momentum. Gary worked his way onto his back and pressed his feet against Benji's chest, then shoved. Benji went flying and landed hard on his back. The wind was sucked out of him, but he was not hurt. He quickly gathered himself, leaped to his feet, and threw himself back onto Gary's chest.

They fought some more.

It was not long until Benji was exhausted. He pushed Gary away and rolled back onto his feet. His jaw pulsated. His neck stiffened. He looked down at his hands and noticed his knuckles were cut and bloodied. Then he looked back up and was greeted by a fist to the mouth, which knocked him back to the floor.

Benji made a cup under his chin and caught the blood. He felt something sharp on his tongue and spit it into the makeshift cup. He recognized what it what right away. "You broke my tooth, you dick!"

"Good," Gary said. He panted like a dog and wiped his lip with the side of his hand. Blood trickled down his face.

For a few seconds, all Benji heard was Gary's heavy breathing, and his own. Until he heard whimpering. Still on the floor, he turned and faced Sheila, and saw that she was crying. She was on the floor now too, her knees pulled up to her chest. Her eyes were wide with fear. Benji followed her gaze and saw it too.

Patricia stood with her feet shoulder width apart, her arms outstretched in front of her. Gary's gun was in her hands. The empty room suddenly fell silent.

This was not good. Patricia was a ticking time bomb, ironically, who could go off at any time. He would never admit it, but Benji was afraid of her. After seeing what she tried to do to her husband out of greed and spite and who knew what else, and how she threw him and Sheila to the side as if trash, she was as ruthless of a person as he had ever met. And now she had a gun.

"Patricia, put the gun down," Gary said. His voice was unusually calm, his tone gentle.

"No."

"What are you going to do with that? Just put it down."

"Shut up."

"Give me the gun."

"Shut up!" She pointed it directly at Gary.

"Patricia, think about what you're doing. We've gotten this far. Let's just finish what we came here to do and head back home."

Patricia kept the gun on him, but her expression softened. Gary must have saw it too because he pressed on.

"It's you and me now," he said to her. "Just like it's always been. Remember why you're here. Who brought you here? Me. Remember? I got you out so you could help me, because I know how smart you are, how valuable. And look, we've done it! We've got them. Just like I said we would.

"Nobody else has to get hurt here. We had to do what we had to do, and now we're here. All I have to do is make one phone call and arrange a trade. We give them Sheila and we get our money. Then it's all over. Just put down the gun."

None of this was news to Benji. That was, in fact, the plan. Whoever Gary actually worked for wanted Sheila for whatever reason, and his job all along had been to capture her and deliver her to those people. Whoever they were. In exchange, Gary would receive a large sum of money, amount undisclosed, to which he would give some to Patricia and some to Benji. It was the same thing in Fiji, except it would have been Randolph receiving the money instead of Patricia.

Benji was naïve, but not that naïve. He knew the odds of actually seeing any money were low, but he had no other option. It was either help Gary and maybe find a way out, or not and rot in jail. At least having a chance, however slim, was better than no chance at all. He wondered if Patricia was smart enough to realize that too.

She lowered the gun.

Gary walked toward her with an extended arm and took the gun from her, then put his arm around her shoulder. Just when it looked like the tension in Patricia's body had fallen away, Gary kept moving his arm around her until it was all the way around her neck. He pressed the gun against her temple.

Benji dropped his head.

"Stupid bitch," Gary said.

•    •    •    •    •

Some time had passed. Benji and Patricia now joined Sheila against the wall, all of their hands bound behind their backs— Benji and Patricia's with twine, Sheila and Randolph's still with zip ties, as they had been when Benji first saw them. Randolph still had not awoken. Gary was in and out of the building, doing whatever it was that people like Gary did. Benji still did not have a read on the man, after everything they had been through. Which meant he was completely in the dark as to what might happen next.

"You know we're fucked, right?" Benji said to the room, not expecting a response.

"Not helpful," Sheila said.

That was it for a while. The more he thought about what to do next, the less he had any idea. It was like a writer's block, except he was not a writer.

Later, when the silence was making him crazy, he said, "You know, in another circumstance, the four of us in this room together might be kind of funny."

"Stop talking," Sheila said.

"It's not funny right now, I'm just saying. It could be funny."

Sheila looked at him with desperate, broken eyes. "Please stop. Please."

He did. Besides, there was nothing else to say. It felt like they were waiting to die. The only mystery in it was which one of them would be first.

To their relief—or at least Benji and surely Sheila's— Randolph finally stirred next to them. Benji felt a rush of excitement knowing he was okay, and Sheila wailed in joy. Nothing from Patricia.

"What's going on?" Randolph managed. His voice was strained. Speaking sounded painful.

"How do you feel?" Sheila said through happy tears. She scooted toward him as much she could without using her useless hands. "How's your head? Can you sit up?"

"Give the man a minute to breathe, will you?" Benji said to her.

Randolph craned his neck and looked at him. "It's nice to you, Benji. About what happened—"

"Don't." Benji suddenly felt an unexpected lump in his throat.

Randolph nodded in response. He grunted.

"Be careful!" Sheila said. She used her shoulder to help Randolph sit up a bit.

Despite the scenario—tied hands, lovers and ex-lovers, attempted murderers and backstabbers—Benji felt a pang of happiness. Seeing Randolph again made his heart feel full. And seeing how Sheila treated him, how much she clearly cared for him, changed his perspective on things a bit. As unorthodox as it may have been, as unlikely as their relationship was, could it be possible they were made for each other? The universe did strange things. It did not seem that hard to believe that the universe linked all of them together for a reason, to help them find where they were supposed to be. Like him with Justice.

*Justice.*

They never would have met otherwise. If they ever got out of here, he would fly back to Fiji and pour his heart out to her. He wanted to be wherever Justice was. That was where he belonged—with her.

He could not help but feel bad for Patricia, as unfathomable as it may have been. She may have brought them all together in the worst of circumstances, but if it was not for her, none of them would be where they were.

Their feet were close, so Benji nudged hers with his. She looked at him and he said, "You okay?"

She nodded but did not say anything.

He could only imagine what was going through her head right now. Frankly, he did not want to know.

"Where's Gary?" Randolph asked as he came-to.

"Don't know," Sheila said. "He's been gone for a while."

"I shouldn't have done that. Challenged him like that. I put everyone at risk."

"No. No, that's not true. Thank you for what you did. Thank you for standing up for me."

It was then Randolph looked at Benji again with curiosity, as if a realization hit him. "What happened to you? Are you missing a tooth?"

Benji almost laughed. He opened his mouth to show off his new smile. Although the bleeding had stopped, his face still ached something fierce.

"I know this might be weird timing," Randolph said, "but anyone see a bathroom around here? I really have to pee."

Benji did laugh this time, even though everything hurt—his face, certainly, but also his ribs and his back and his head. It was well worth it. Having Randolph back in his life felt so good. He missed him.

But the joy did not last long.

Just then, on the other side of the big, empty room, the door opened. Benji tensed as a shadow walked through the doorway. When the shadow came into view, Sheila sprang to her feet as if set on fire and shrieked so loudly, Benji thought his eardrums might explode. He did not know who the person was, but what he did know was that it was not Gary, and that made him as happy as he had been in a very, very long time.

# CHAPTER TWENTY-TWO

*Five years ago.* Sheila thought about baby Minka every day for five years. Even as she trekked across Europe making new acquaintances, holding the occasional odd job, and never staying in one place too long, her sister was always on her mind. Especially during the hard days when she was hungry or cold or rundown or afraid. On those days, she thought of baby Minka and what she might be like as a little kid rather than the toddler she remembered. She imagined what her voice might sound like, and her laugh. She wondered what her favorite toys were, and if she still remembered her sister Sheila. On the very worst of days, she thought about their father and what he might do to Minka when she got older, and it helped get her through. Motivation was a beautiful thing, and that motivation was what helped her survive.

Everywhere she went, Sheila bought a postcard. Which meant after five years, she had a stack of postcards so thick, the elastic band she used to keep them together had nearly snapped. The problem was, she could not send the postcards to the house in Sweden, or her father would know where she was. Not to mention, Minka was only a small child who probably could not yet read. So Sheila collected the postcards, wrote a short note on each, and kept them. That way, once Minka got a little older, Sheila could send them all to her somehow and show her the journey and make sure she would never forget that her big sister loved her more than anything in the world.

Sheila spent a year in western Poland where she worked on an assembly line at a paper manufacturing facility. It was the most mundane, mindless job she could imagine, but it gave her a lot of time to think. She stopped getting calluses on her fingers after the first month, and from there spent day after day doing the same thing repeatedly, all while plotting out her next move. Money had run low by then, so she roomed with three other women in a tiny apartment in the city to save as much money as possible. During that time, she grew to love pierogies with all types of filling—from chocolate to raspberries to kielbasa. She often ate them three times a day and almost never got tired of them. Even if she had, she would have kept eating them because they were filling and often nutritious, depending on the filling, and relatively inexpensive. After she put ten good pounds on and saved more than enough money to relocate, she did just that.

Two weeks in Berlin, Germany, three months in Prague, Czech Republic, fourteen months in Munich, Germany. She worked many temporary and seasonal jobs and was careful not to get too close to anyone. Once in Munich, she shamefully accepted one thousand euros to spend a single night with a wealthy man in a hotel room. She did things she was not proud of that night, and she wished to forget them forever, but that was all part of it. Whatever it took to survive, she did it. Even still, the shame she felt for months afterward—years even—was tough on her. She questioned her reason for doing what she was doing. She was no better than her father in that way, she thought, since he had prepared to do the same thing. That was the worst part about it, being like him.

She drank heavily for a while after that, for a month or two. The drink did not do much to help her, though, and it quickly got very expensive. Then one night, after two men in a sports car offered to show her their penises in exchange for a bottle of brandy—all she had to do was touch them, they said, but she knew better—she decided it was time to stop drinking—and to leave Germany. The very next morning, she bought a ticket to Liechtenstein and never looked back. It was the last time she ever used her body to earn money; she was determined to find other means, including using her brain. She forwent the postcard and keep that leg of her journey to herself.

In Liechtenstein, she redefined herself. She cleaned up her appearance, bought a bicycle, and began riding around the village in search of work. By then she spoke three languages, including fluent German, and had learned how to use her charm to become friendly with the wealthy families. In a matter of days, she was offered a job as a live-in housekeeper at one of the castles on the hill, and she lived and worked for the family for nearly two full years. She ate well there, slept well, and was paid the best money of her life. She hated leaving them when the time came, but they understood she had places to go, a life to live. Upon her departure, they gave her an envelope filled with enough francs to last her another year, if she was careful with it. Like the man on the boat, Mikael, she would never forget the Buchel family and their hospitality for as long as she lived. They really helped her to reestablish herself and get back on the right track—the path to saving Minka.

The rest of the time she spent in Dublin, Ireland, where she unintentionally fell in love for the first time. His name was Liam, and he was the kindest, most charming, and it turned out, most jealous man she had ever met. What started as a typical romance turned into a flee for her life.

Three weeks prior, Sheila took a walk in the park. It was there she made accidental eye contact with a passerby, who smiled at her in return. She thought nothing of it until a minute later, when someone tapped her on the shoulder.

"Yes?" she said, turning to the person. To him.

"Hi," he said. He stared at her, his mouth partially agape, two big dimples swallowing his face.

"Can I help you?" she said once it got awkward.

He laughed and apologized, said she was the most beautiful woman he had ever laid eyes on, and insisted she join him for coffee and croissants. How could a girl decline such a flattering invitation? Two hours later, they walked hand in hand down the sidewalk. Sheila's stomach was full and her heart fluttered. When they got to her building, Liam did not ask to come up; he did not tell her he had a great time; he did not tell her he wanted to see her again. Instead, he curled his fingers around the back of her neck with the sensuality of a saint and pulled her close, stopping just before their lips touched. He waited for her to fill the gap between them.

Sheila shook all over, from head to toe, including the crevices she was unaware she had. Her knees and her lips and her thighs trembled in the best way possible. She shook until she could not take it anymore, then she pressed down on her toes and closed the gap between them, kissing him with a gentle passion that she only ever saw in films.

They saw each other every day for more than two weeks. To have said it was a whirlwind romance would have been an understatement. From flowers to flirty text messages to expensive dinners to thoughtful handpicked gifts. Then from calls at all hours of the night to having her email hacked to her catching him following her during the day when he should have been at work.

When she tried to break it off, Liam nearly lost his mind. That night, she heard him loitering outside the building through her window, calling her name, though nothing happened. The next night was the same, except this time he had been drinking, which made for a loud, obnoxious night for everyone inside the building. He yelled for her over and over, sometimes calling her untrue foul names, sometimes professing his love for her and begging her for forgiveness. Someone called the Garda and when they showed up, Liam was none too pleased.

"Sheila! You bitch! I'm going to get you for this!"

Sheila stood near the door in her apartment where Liam could not see, wrapped in a blanket, tears streaming down her face. It was not she who called the Garda, but she was too frightened to say anything. Instead, she listened to them fight to take him away.

She had fallen in love with him so fast, yet now she was terrified of him. How did that even happen? It was like she hardly knew him at all, which was actually true. All they knew of each other was on the surface, nothing real. He knew nothing about how she grew up or about her father or baby Minka. All he knew was her name and that she liked to be romanced—which, who did not? She questioned everything after that—what was love, really, and how did it make people do strange things? Was it even love at all with Liam, or was it lust? The ease in which she fell for him and his charm terrified her. It was like she lost herself in the process, and forgot all about what her focus should have been. Minka.

She lost all hope for men after that. Lars and her father and the sailor, and now Liam, too many of the men she met were ugly—but not in the physical sense. And she wanted no part of that. Men would hold her back from her ultimate goal.

She packed all her necessities that night and slept for a few hours. In the morning, she went to the corner store and bought a postcard, then took the first ferry to Liverpool in the United Kingdom. On the way, she called the Buchel's home and thanked Mrs. Buchel for everything she and her family had done for her, and for helping to remind her of who she was. They had a tearful conversation about it, to which Sheila felt so much better afterward.

It was in Liverpool where she decided it was time to act—really act. Five years had passed and she had accomplished nothing aside from bouncing around Europe and barely surviving, not living at all. She was tired of it and needed to do something to change it. So she began plotting her way to the United States, determined to get there, no matter what it took.

# CHAPTER TWENTY-THREE

*Present day.* Randolph was groggy. His thoughts were cloudy. His head was killing him. The headache stretched from his temples to his neck. His everything pulsated. He remembered Gary coming on to Sheila, then he remembered Gary hitting him in the head with something. After that, he did not remember much. Nothing, really. Just blackness.

And now, as he watched Sheila leap to her feet and run across the room toward the person in the doorway, he felt like he was missing something. His view of the doorway was blocked, so all he saw was Sheila's back—and her hands behind it.

The unknown person wrapped their arms around Sheila. Two different people sobbed. Randolph sat where he was with Benji and Patricia, not wanting to interrupt whatever what was happening across the room. As the clouds in his mind parted, he thought he might know who it was, but he tried not to get his hopes up. Considering how they were taken and brought to this place, that seemed unlikely.

Sheila turned back with the person—a woman much younger than her; a girl, really—next to her. The girl had her arm around Sheila's waist. Randolph did not recognize her, but he would not have even if she was who he thought she was. He tried to stand up but struggled.

"Let me help you," the girl said, running over to him.

He did not realize just how young she was until she got closer. She was tall like a full-grown woman, but had childlike features and was thin like someone who needed time to fill out their frame. The girl slipped her arms under his armpits and lifted on the count of three.

His knees wobbled at first, but he quickly settled and composed himself.

"Are you okay?" the young, thin girl asked him.

He nodded. "Thank you."

The girl smiled quickly but did not otherwise acknowledge him.

"How old are you?" Randolph asked. She could not have been more than fourteen, maybe sixteen on her best day.

Sheila stepped forward and said, "Randolph, this is her. This is my sister."

"I'm Minka," the girl, Sheila's sister, said.

Minka. The person who was behind all this, the reason for Sheila doing everything she did. The person Sheila was here to protect.

"I've heard so much about you," Randolph said. "And I'd love to chat, but . . . any chance you have something to cut us free?"

Minka smiled and Sheila laughed.

"Will this work?" Minka pulled out a switchblade.

Relief flooded through him. "I think you're my hero."

Each of them turned and showed Minka their backs. One by one, she cut them free. When the zip tie snapped and his wrists were free, it felt like a weight fell off his body. The blood rushed to his wrists and fingers and made them tingle. He shook them out until all the sensation returned again. Burn-like marks covered his wrists where the plastic had dug into his skin.

Instead of a celebratory feeling, the energy in the room became awkward. They were one group of people but clearly with different agendas—three against two—and what to do next was not clear.

"So," Benji said, seemingly sensing the same issue, "I don't want to be the asshole, but now what?"

Nobody answered.

"And dare I ask, where's Gary?"

Right, Gary. Randolph was so blinded by the excitement of the pending freedom that he completely forgot about that part of the situation. Where was Gary?

"I don't know about you guys, but I don't really want to find out," Benji said. "I'm going to get the hell out of here before he comes back." Benji did not wait for a response; he started for the door.

"If by Gary you mean that loser outside with the unloaded gun, then don't worry about him," Minka said.

"The gun wasn't even loaded?" Benji said. "You've got to be shitting me."

On one hand, Randolph felt relieved. On the other, he was embarrassed. It was four of them and one of Gary. If only they had known that the gun was not even loaded, they could have overpowered him before, instead of what happened. Did that mean nothing happened when he shot at the ceiling? Randolph thought it had, but perhaps it was just the anticipation of it that had spooked him into thinking there was.

"How do you know the gun wasn't loaded?" Sheila asked.

Minka smiled with crooked teeth, a couple of them only partially grown in, and shrugged. "Lucky, I guess?"

• • • • •

Minka went on to tell them the story. She was on the way to the meet up location Sheila had set up when she received a text message from her sister—an SOS, more like it—asking if she was in a white sedan, by chance. She was not. It was then Minka knew something had gone awry. She and Sheila each downloaded an app on their phones which would track the other's location, so it was as simple as opening that and following the dot. Minka rerouted the cab driver and did just that.

She had the driver drop her off a quarter-mile from where the dot stopped moving, and she covered the rest of the distance on foot so to be inconspicuous. She was not exactly sure what to expect, or where she was headed.

Sheila's location brought her outside a rusty red brick building with broken windows and no signs of life anytime in the last decade. Which seemed like the perfect location to try to hide someone. Armed with only a switchblade for protection, Minka kept tight against the building and walked slowly. One small step at a time. One step, pause to listen for anything. Another step, pause and listen again. At some point, she heard a commotion on the inside of the building but failed to make out what it was. She creeped as close to the corner of the building as she could without exposing herself to what might be on the other side—or who.

Before long, the sound of a door opening made her freeze, and she held her position with her back against the brick. She worked up the courage to look once she heard a voice talking then pause, then talk some more. Since there was only one voice, she figured the voice—a man's—was talking on the phone. And maybe, if she was lucky, he was distracted.

She saw a body on the ground with a red puddle around him, and she froze again and questioned if she was strong enough, and clever enough, to outsmart a grown adult man. She wanted to give herself credit for running away from home without getting caught, but in reality, all she did was follow the directions, step by step, that Sheila had sent to her.

Just when she doubted she could do it, when she thought about turning back and quitting, she thought about Sheila and all she had done for her. It started with postcards with short notes explaining to Minka who her sister was and why she left. Eventually that led to longer letters requiring a secret decoder to help unscramble the gibberish. It was all for protection, Sheila explained once. If their mother or father found out they were communicating, Sheila said their father would send people after her. Whatever that meant. But Minka believed her, so she did what she asked. She trusted Sheila.

Which was why it was her turn to look out for her sister, since she was in trouble. That was what sisters did.

Minka took a deep breath, quietly, and kept walking toward the man on the phone with tiny steps. His back was to her as he spoke then listened, then spoke some more. When she was close enough to make out every word he said, she stood and waited. And listened.

"I've got her, I'm telling you," the man said. "What more proof do you want?"

Then after a few seconds: "I don't give a shit what you do with her. You bring the cash, you can have the girl."

Then: "Even if I wanted to, I can't. All I've got is blanks anyway. Besides, even if I could, what good would I be to you anymore if I did? The order was to bring her alive. That's exactly what I've done. And now you pay up or I take the girl somewhere and the pay is double."

Then: "You better tell that asshole I mean it. And you can tell him I said that."

The man hung up the phone after that and slipped it into his pocket. Minka knew this was her one and maybe only chance.

"Mister?"

He turned around so fast she thought he might fall over. "What the? How long have you been standing there?"

"Do you have a bathroom I can use?"

"What?"

"A bathroom?" She crossed her legs and bounced up and down for effect. "It's an emergency."

"No bathroom here. Scram."

"Please."

The man sighed and stepped toward her. He looked past her as if he expected to see someone, an adult maybe. But he would find no one. It was just them.

"Where'd you even come from?" he asked. "How'd you get here?"

Minka did not respond. She had not prepared that far in advance.

The man looked at her for a long few seconds. Then, as if hit by a realization, his eyes slowly opened wider and wider. "Do I know you?"

"No."

He shook his head. "No, I think I do. Yeah, yeah, I definitely do. You're . . . you're that girl."

"No, I'm not."

The man smiled a creepy smile now. "This must be my lucky day. Two-for-one special, coming right up." He reached forward to grab her, and her training kicked in.

The one extracurricular activity her parents allowed her to partake in was martial arts. There was a grate in the floor of her bedroom where she could sometimes hear her parents talking about adult topics. Once it was about martial arts.

"What do you think?" her mother asked her father that night.

"Might be a good idea," he said. "Just in case some of my guys get a little handsy. You know how they can be sometimes."

The next morning, her mother told her she would begin taking martial arts classes. Little did they know, she was a natural.

As soon as the man in front of her reached for her, Minka swung down on his forearm to block him. With her other hand, she grabbed his wrist and yanked, and she immediately pulled him forward. She twisted his wrist until he screamed in pain, then she slid her foot under his ankles and swiped as hard as she could. The man fell onto his chest like a sack of rocks. Minka quickly leaped on his back, driving her knees into his kidneys, and slid an arm under his chin.

While in training, she was told to never use submission techniques unless she was in danger. Now, she thought, she was definitely in danger; a situation like this was exactly what it was all for. She hoped her instructor would not be angry with her if he found out. With one hand still under his chin, she made her other arm into a V and placed her palm on the back of his head. Then with pressure from the back arm against the pressure from the front arm, she squeezed.

She closed her eyes and counted to ten—not a second longer—and released. The man fell limp underneath her. Then without needing to think about it, she immediately slid off him before he woke up. While she watched him talk on the phone, she noticed a line of twine dangling out of his back pocket. And considering how thick the bump in his pocket was, she risked that there was still a lot left.

And there was.

She reached for the ball of twine and pulled it out. Quickly and efficiently, she grabbed his wrists and pulled them behind his back, then grabbed an ankle and pulled it as far as it could go. Within seconds, the man was hogtied with both wrists and both ankles behind his back, and would be entirely unable to move once he regained consciousness. Which would not be long.

Hogtying was another trick Minka had learned, just not in martial arts. For that, she could thank her friend Valeria, whose family had a pig farm.

Being an almost grown up was kind of fun.

# CHAPTER TWENTY-FOUR

*Present day.* Benji stood there, his mouth partially agape, in complete admiration of the girl in front of him. "How old did you say you were?" he asked her.

"Thirteen."

He was baffled. Thirteen? At thirteen, he was playing video games all day and snacking on cheese-flavored corn chips instead of studying like he was supposed to. But this girl—at thirteen!—just beat the shit out of a grown man and tied him up like a farm animal. By herself.

Badass.

"I'm so proud of you," Sheila said. It was clear she was. Her eyes were moist as she pulled her sister into an embrace and squeezed.

"Any idea who he was talking to?" Randolph asked now.

Patricia still had not said a word.

"No," Minka said.

"I do," Sheila said.

All eyes in the room landed on her.

"I don't have time to explain right now, but trust me, we need to get out of here."

Silence.

"Gary called it in, so they're already on the way. Let's hope they weren't close."

"What do they want?" Randolph asked her as if he already knew who they were.

"What do you think they want? They want what they've always wanted. Me. And now, her." She meant Minka.

"What do we do?" Randolph asked.

"We run."

•　　•　　•　　•　　•

The light was so bright it nearly blinded Benji when he stepped outside. Which, of course, led to him stepping directly into the pool of blood surrounding the dead man. Naturally. A few feet to his right was Gary, his hands and feet tied behind his back just like Minka had described.

"Hey!" Gary called out from the ground, apparently conscious again. "Hey!"

Benji walked around him, sticky shoes and all, and looked down at Gary. He looked pathetic and desperate, having been hogtied by a teenage girl. And Benji loved that.

"Benjamin, thank god! Help me out of this, will you? One second I was talking on the phone, the next I was blindsided and tripped, then tied. Can you believe that?"

"I don't think so."

"Untie me, right now!"

Benji bent down so he was eye level with the man who had put him through so much bullshit, so he could get a good look at him. "I hope you rot in hell."

Benji ignored Gary's response, which was that of a toddler throwing a tantrum.

He was joined outside by Randolph and Sheila, and her sister the badass. Patricia was last out.

"I don't see anyone," Sheila said as she scanned the horizon. "Which means we still have time, but we need to get out of here, like now."

"I saw a row of trees over there," Minka said, pointing somewhere Benji did not see but imagined was the same area he saw when they arrived. "Might be a way out."

"Let's go," Sheila said, and she took off running in that direction. Minka was on her hip.

Randolph stayed where he was, seemingly torn about what he should do. Sheila turned around and called after him, but kept running.

"What are you doing?" Benji said to him. "Why aren't you running?"

"Benji, I—"

"Just go, man. Save yourself."

"What about you?"

Benji felt that lump in his throat again. It kept him from vocalizing a response, so he just shrugged.

"Come with us," Randolph said.

"What?"

"I'm serious."

Sheila called Randolph's name again. Her voice echoed off the broken building.

"But what about—"

"But nothing. I know it wasn't personal. You did what you had to do, just like I did. Come with us."

Benji did not know what to say. This was unexpected. For all he had been through in his life, Randolph reaching out to him like this might have been the nicest thing anyone had ever done for him. Ever. Was this what it felt like to be cared about?

His mind was made up. Hell to the yes.

Benji began running, but suddenly stopped in his tracks as a thought crossed his mind. He turned back and saw Patricia, who looked defeated and lonely. Sad. Her eyes faced the ground.

"Hold up a second," Benji said. He ran over to her. "Hey."

She looked up. Tears filled her eyes.

"I know things didn't go exactly as planned, but I just wanted to say I'm sorry. For everything."

She nodded in acceptance but did not say anything.

"What are you going to do?"

"I've realized a few things about myself," she said, "and none of them are good. I think I know where I belong after all this. And it's not out here. There's no need to fight it anymore."

"But, here?"

"I'm tired of running. I'm tired of trying to be someone I'm not. Whatever happens to me at this point, happens."

Benji felt uneasy about it. It felt too easy. Nothing with Patricia had been easy.

"Don't worry," she said, seeing something on his face that showed his doubts. "I won't mention your name. If anything, I'll take all the blame. It was me and Gary, only us. You getting mixed up in it was all just a big misunderstanding."

Benji did not know what to say. None of the logistics made much sense to him right now, but he did not have time to dwell on the specifics. He stepped toward Patricia and pulled her into an embrace. It took a few seconds, but she eventually reciprocated. Her warmth blended into his, and it reminded him of what their relationship used to be like, of how everything began.

That was before.

Now was after.

Here it ends.

And it was what happened now that mattered, not before. It seemed everyone knew that and agreed.

They separated. Patricia offered him a sad but definitive smile as his parting gift. He got the impression he may never see her again, or at least not as a free woman.

Benji turned his back to her and prepared to chase after the others, and as he did, he locked onto Randolph. He and Patricia looked at one another. Benji bounced his eyes from him to her, from her to him, and saw nothing. No expression. No emotion. No regret. All he saw was finality between them, closure about everything that had happened. Patricia nodded once and Randolph returned it, and that felt like enough—at least to Benji. Their history was their own, though, and he wanted no part of it anymore.

"You ready?" he said to Randolph.

"Ready."

"Are you sure?"

"Positive."

Benji nodded. Then without looking back, he turned his shoulders and sprinted toward Sheila and Minka, who had since stopped and were waiting. It was not long before Randolph caught up and they all ran together.

As they crossed the threshold of the trees, a dark SUV skidded into the sandy parking lot and screeched to a stop near where Patricia remained, along with the dead body and hogtied Gary, a massive sand cloud forming over them. What would happen next, Benji would never know, and he told himself he would not care. And as the four of them hurried under the protection of nature's canopy, he actually believed it.

# CHAPTER TWENTY-FIVE

*Two years ago.* Getting into the United States was one thing—not that difficult, Sheila learned—but progressing from there was far more challenging. She had no family in the States and was unmarried. She failed to meet the qualifications of a refugee and was without a career worthy of receiving a green card—in fact, she had no career at all.

She bounced around from place to place, state to state, living the nomad life like she had in Europe. She took odd jobs for cash under the table at first, all of which helped her pay for temporary housing for months at a time. But she grew tired of that life—of the constant moving and feeling of being unsettled. She wanted and knew she had to do things the right way and follow the laws of the country she so desperately wanted to start a new life in, so she did. She found herself a reputable immigration attorney and got all her ducks in a row, so to speak.

Whether it was luck or just being in the right place at the right time, there was a code in the immigration laws that favored victims of trafficking. Her attorney handled everything while she laid low, and after meetings upon meetings with the immigration office where she recounted her story, Sheila was eventually granted a green card, which opened up so many more opportunities for her. Real jobs. Apartments. A bank account. It changed everything.

There was nothing glamorous about her new life in the United States. The jobs she found paid poorly and her expenses most often cost more than her income. She held multiple jobs at a time to make ends meet while always seeming to move north— first a hotel housekeeper and a telephone customer service representative for a telecommunications company in Houston, Texas; then a retail worker and farmhand in Sun City, Kansas, where it was as hot as the name implied; and a custodian at an elementary school and an assistant for a borderline shady real estate agent in St. Louis, Missouri—that was until she found a job waiting tables at a Mexican restaurant in Springfield, Illinois, and made more money working that one job than she had working two at a time in the other places.

It was a difficult existence. She ate lots of cheap pasta and drank water from the tap. But she had a larger vision in mind, and it was all part of the journey. All the while, she kept so busy just trying to survive and was preoccupied and focused on the task at hand, that she completely forgot about creepy Liam from Dublin. Staying away from men entirely during that time only helped her, she thought, and it was a justification for doing so. That logic did not apply to women, however. With women, she could be whoever she wanted to be and have fun and get her needs met, because women knew what other women wanted, without worrying about everything else. That was a different story, though. What could she say? She had needs, just as everyone did.

Sheila wasted three years of her life just surviving, biding time until Minka was a little older and more capable of understanding. There was one day a year where sending something to her parents' house in Sweden would not raise eyebrows, one time a year where she might be able to slip something through without them noticing.

Might.

But she had to risk it.

Minka's eleventh birthday. It was the only time of year a child could receive mail without drawing suspicion. Between aunts and grandparents and cousins and maybe a pen pal or an old classmate who moved away, a child receiving scattered pieces of mail for a few days on either side of their birthday would be expected.

It was Sheila's chance to cash in all those postcards.

What was special about Minka's eleventh birthday? That was how old Sheila was when she started making deliveries for her father. Which meant Sheila's notes would make sense once Minka had to start working for the family business too. A year earlier and she might not believe a word about the information Sheila would be giving her. And if Minka mentioned anything to their parents about it, it would have been game over for Sheila.

So she waited until then, as much as it killed her.

The drop-offs were risky but not overtly dangerous most of the time. Aside from the occasional creepy man who wanted more than what her father put in her backpack, most men were satisfied with the contraband. As sad as it made her to think about, Minka could handle those transactions. Sheila had. It was what would come four years later that would completely destroy her innocence—a feeling Sheila knew all too well. And that was if their father had the patience to wait that long for Minka to grow. Or worse, if Minka's body decided it was time before her mind could handle it.

Three days before Minka's eleventh birthday, Sheila gathered all her postcards, each with a short note describing her journey, and wrapped a handful of elastic bands around them. Keeping them in order was critical. The notes were in chronological order, so by doing so, if Minka read them in order, she could paint a picture of what Sheila was telling her. And it would show her Sheila's journey visually—from city to city, country to country—as a way to show Minka how far Sheila was willing to travel for her. The most important thing was that Minka knew, without a doubt, that Sheila never forgot about her. That was the only way it would ever work.

Sheila brought the banded postcards to the post office downtown and sealed them in a small box. She paid extra for a guaranteed delivery across the globe in one to three days.

Then she waited.

An agonizing week went by, then another, then another. By the time the fourth week ended and she had not heard from the police or her father, she finally began to relax. By not hearing from anyone, she figured Minka had received the package, read the postcards, and understood how important it was to keep it to herself. They still had so far to go, so long of a journey, but it was a critical first step.

The last line of the final postcard said that Minka was to wait to hear from Sheila with the next steps. A few weeks later, Sheila mailed an envelope to Sweden—to Minka's school—where her parents would not see it. It was not easy, though. Students could not receive mail at school, so Sheila called the school one day pretending to be their mother, and begged them to allow it. She could not say why, she told the school, but it was a matter of personal safety and was regarding Minka's father. As part of the agreement, the school was to, under no circumstances, call the house to discuss the matter and keep all communication through email to maintain Minka's safety. The correspondence went to an inbox Sheila monitored, of course.

The risk was enormous, but Sheila saw no other alternative. She knew the school would involve the authorities and begin an investigation into their father, hopefully quietly. How long that investigation might take was anyone's guess. This one time, Sheila hoped her father's secretive dealings were just that—truly secretive—and difficult to uncover so she would have time to get Minka out. If it was the opposite, the odds were that Sheila would get exposed.

Sheila was careful not to trust the school. Since they were certainly working with the police and would share information with them to assist in their investigation into her father, Sheila's first letter to Minka at the school would be undetectable. As part of her final postcard, she gave Minka a decoder—although an eleven-year-old would not have known what it was—with the letters of the alphabet and a corresponding number. But instead of a traditional one through twenty-six assignment for the letters—one representing A, twenty-six representing Z—Sheila randomized it. For protection.

While an eleven-year-old would not be able to figure it out at first glance, the professionals might be able to, even without the decoder. Without any pattern at all, Sheila had assigned each letter a random number—thirteen for A, seven for B, and so on—so that Minka would need to use the decoder from the postcard to translate the message. Which also meant if the authorities tried to intercept the message and decode it using the traditional one through twenty-six method, it would be complete gibberish. As long as Minka kept the decoder safe and to herself, she could safely and privately read Sheila's messages and follow her instructions.

It went on like that for nearly two full years. Sheila would send sporadic notes with details about what Minka was to do. The problem was, Sheila had no way of knowing that Minka understood the messages and did what she asked of her. The risk was too great to have Minka send anything to Sheila as confirmation or otherwise—that would have involved Sheila sharing her address, which would not have worked if she wanted to stay hidden.

So Sheila spent almost two years sending her sister messages, blindly hoping she would understand. And despite that reality, she always knew, deep inside her soul, that Minka did understand. Call it a sister's intuition or call it *naivety*, but somehow Sheila knew everything would be okay, that somehow they would be together again someday.

And it turned out, she was right.

# CHAPTER TWENTY-SIX

*Present day.* Randolph's lungs burned as he followed the others into the shade. As much as it hurt, the tires grinding over the tiny pebbles at his back helped him push through; it was catch up or be left behind, though not really. Sheila turned back what seemed like every few steps, as did Benji, to check on him. Randolph did not have the wind to assure them he was okay, so he waved instead. They kept going.

They ran for a while, or jogged, the pace slowing. For a long while. Until suddenly, they stopped. At some point, both Sheila and Minka pulled up at nearly the same time, as if their bodies were in sync. Randolph was completely relieved, his everything desperate for a break. He was not sure how much more running he had left in him before his body gave out; it had been decades since the last time he ran. He nearly crashed into a tree as he tried to slow down, then wrapped his arms around it and collapsed.

Breathe in, breathe out. Repeat.

Breathe in, breathe out.

Before long, his lungs recovered and he could breathe close to normally again, and he felt the oxygen fuel his muscles and replenish his soul.

Benji stood over him and held out his hand. Randolph grabbed it at let the much younger—though maybe not stronger, but definitely in better shape—man pull him to his feet.

"You okay, old man?"

"I'm good."

Benji chuckled and patted Randolph's back.

"I think we're safe now," Minka said, hardly sucking wind at all.

"For now," Sheila said.

There was something in her tone, something dark and irritable, that struck Randolph as off. There was something she was not telling them, and he wanted to know what it was. He tried to catch her eye, to share a silent moment to show her it would be okay, but she would not look at him. She would not look at anyone, it seemed.

"Sheila?" he said to her finally when the silent communication did not work.

She turned and showed him the blankness in her eyes, the nothingness. It scared him.

"What is it?" he asked.

The others faced her.

"What's wrong?"

"It's just . . . this is bad. Really, really, bad. Way worse than I thought. Damn! I should have seen it coming."

"What are you talking about?" Randolph pressed, now concerned.

"Gary."

"Don't worry about him anymore. Did you not see what your sister did to him? Gary's gone now, out of our lives for good."

"It's not that. It's not about Gary."

Randolph was confused. "You're not making any sense. You just said—"

"Listen," Sheila said as she began pacing, "I just figured it all out. I'm so pissed! I can't believe this is actually happening. I realized it could but hoped it wouldn't. This wasn't part of the plan! This was the one scenario I dreaded and didn't have a way out. I hate to say it, but I think we're all royally screwed."

Now Randolph was really worried. Like he could feel his heart in his chest worried.

"Gary isn't who he said he is," Sheila went on, which made Randolph hold his breath. "The reason we're here, in Palau, was because the island isn't a member of INTERPOL. Which means, if what Gary said was true about working for them, he wouldn't have any jurisdiction at all. He couldn't touch me here."

Randolph's mind spun.

"But he's here. And based on what Minka overheard, that doesn't sound like someone talking to someone at an international government agency, does it?"

Hard to argue that point.

"Which means?" Randolph said.

"Which means he doesn't work for INTERPOL. And if it's not INTERPOL looking for me, it could only be one other person."

"Dad," Minka said with sadness, seeming to understand what Sheila was getting at.

"Exactly."

The blow struck Randolph where it counted.

"So you're telling me," Benji said in a condescending tone, "that Gary's been working with your dad this whole time?"

Sheila nodded. "That's exactly what I'm saying."

"You've got to be fucking kidding me!" Immediately after Benji said it, he winced and turned to Minka and apologized. She waved it off.

Everything was moving too fast for Randolph to process. None of it made any sense.

"Which, if I'm being frank," Sheila said, "is the worst possible case scenario. Because if he's working for my father, the only possible reason he wants me back is that he wants to get even. I left and ruined his business, and his life, and he was pissed. And now he wants me to pay for it."

"I, um," Minka began slowly, sounding unsure of herself, "there's something I haven't had time to tell you yet."

"What is it?" Sheila asked her sister.

"I didn't forget, I just . . . there was never a good time because we've been—"

"Minka, it's okay. I'm not mad at you, but I need to know."

"It's about Dad."

"What about him?"

"He's gone."

"Gone? What does that mean?"

"They got him."

Sheila looked to be in awe, speechless. And she was. Randolph thought his head might pop off.

"Prison," Minka added, as if it was needed. "They arrested him three days before I left."

# CHAPTER TWENTY-SEVEN

*Present day.* While many thoughts and feelings ravaged through Benji's mind and body, the most prominent one was anger. He was pissed at Gary. If what Sheila said was true, that meant Gary had never worked for INTERPOL and had no authority to do anything he did—most notably, getting Benji released from jail. How did that make any sense? Benji was no longer in jail, was he not?

Between all the access Gary had demonstrated to have had—the tracking technology on Randolph and Sheila; the connections at the airport; the seemingly endless amount of personal information he had on Sheila; the official-looking blue notice form from INTERPOL Benji saw with his own two eyes, for Christ's sake!—Benji had a hard time connecting those dots. How was it possible that Gary had all that and more, and was not somehow associated with INTERPOL? Benji allowed for the possibility that maybe it was not INTERPOL exactly, but it had to have been an organization like it.

Benji had a different thought. An alternative scenario that may have been even worse than the one Sheila presented. The more he thought about the facts and considered it, the more plausible it became. With the plausibility came the impact of that scenario, and what that could mean for them all.

And it was not good.

They were all, indeed, royally screwed—and that was being generous.

Benji had thoughts of sharing his actual worst-case scenario with the group, but as he observed them all slowly crumbling before him, he held his tongue. Sheila had begun to sob. Benji felt for what she was going through. She had made it so far, came so close to getting away and rescuing her sister, and had come up just short. Climbing to the top of the mountain only to fall all the way back to the base was enough to completely destroy someone's psyche, even the strong ones. It seemed to him that Sheila may have been experiencing that devastation right now.

Next to her was her badass sister, the martial arts prodigy, looking every much the thirteen-year-old girl she was—tall yet tiny, shrunken shoulders, an expression bordering on weepy that looked like it might give way at any second. Because that was exactly what she was—a girl. And girls were not supposed to know how to handle the stress of a situation like this. Lots of adults did not even know.

And Randolph—poor, poor Randolph. It seemed like he hardly knew what to do with himself. Sheila was on her backside on the ground now, with her face in her hands and her emotions seeping out the crevices of her fingers. He put a hand on her shoulder as a way of comfort and reassurance, but Sheila did not—could not—even acknowledge him. Meanwhile, a young girl stood next to him, teetering herself, and she was just a girl. Benji watched Randolph try to stretch his limbs beyond their capabilities and comfort both ladies at the same time, torn between being a good partner and reacting with the fatherly instincts Benji knew existed from personal experience. One second he crouched to show Sheila he was there; the next he tentatively wrapped his arm around Minka as if asking permission, then pulled her close into a side hug. Benji would have had to have been a monster to interrupt the scene with even worse news.

So he did not.

He bit his lip until the words burrowed back into their home in his head while he helplessly stood in place and tried not to make anything worse. He thought about Justice just then, and realized he missed her so much that it pained him—physically hurt. Her smile bounced through his mind like a love song on repeat and made him so happy, yet also so sad at the same time. Despite their current outlook looking maybe as grim as it ever had, he still felt that he would find a way out, that he would find a way to see her again.

The grinding and snapping of the forest pulled him from his trance. He refocused and looked at the group to see if they heard what he did, but they were all still struggling as they had been before.

More grinding.

More snapping.

Then came the gentle hum of what sounded like an engine.

Benji stiffened and quickly looked around in all directions, his eyes darting from one part of the forest to the other in a flash. Nothing. But then the grinding and snapping and humming got louder, and closer, and he knew he could not have imagined it.

Randolph stood up tall and looked around too, then found Benji's eyes. "Do you hear that?"

Benji nodded and held a finger to his lips.

Sheila magically stopped crying and stood up, and she put herself in front of Minka just like one might expect a big sister to do.

They all listened.

Through a clearing not far from where they were, an ATV sped toward them. Benji watched, unmoving, unthinking, as the vehicle grew larger and larger as it seemed to pick up speed.

Where the clearing widened, two more ATVs appeared from behind the first, then a fourth, and they formed a line as they approached.

Was it possible a rescue team had been sent to save them? Although, from what? Did police ride ATVs in Palau? Oh, maybe it was just a group of friends enjoying some leisure time in the forest!

Or, maybe it was exactly who Benji knew—who they all knew—it would be.

The four ATVs pulled up in front of them. The drivers, all men hidden behind sunglasses, leaped off and withdrew weapons from behind their backs. Guns, of course, because it was always guns. Benji made a mental note that maybe he should get a gun one of these days too—you know, as protection, since he kept finding himself in situations like this where having one would be handy.

That was if he lived beyond today.

The man in the front kept his weapon up as he walked toward the girls. Two things stood out right away. First was that the barrel of the gun was not pointed in the general direction of the girls, but rather directly at Sheila. Not good. Second was that he, and all three other drivers, had scalps so clean Benji could almost see his reflection on them. It was awfully similar to how the men in the cave looked in Fiji, and the not-actually-a-limo-driver-but-pretending-to-be-one driver who brought them to the cave.

And by similar, it was the same. Benji knew.

Crips.

Unlike earlier where it was one man, Gary, and one gun against four with zero guns, this time Benji would not try to play the hero. The guns the four skinheads held were not handguns; they were assault rifles. Which meant they were not just there to kill, they were there to annihilate.

"My, my, my, look who it is," the skinhead in front of Sheila said. The rifle was mere inches from her face. "The one and only

Sheila Backe. You wouldn't believe the bullshit your father's put us through to find you."

Her father? It had been established, theoretically, that her father was after her, but the Crips? What did the Crips have to do with her father?

"I've got to say," the man continued, "I'm almost impressed how long you managed to stay away. Almost." The man smirked. "Round 'em up, boys."

With that, each man approached one person each—Benji, Randolph, and Minka—while the speaking man grabbed Sheila's shoulder and spun her around. Benji felt a yank on his wrist then heard the zipping of a plastic tie as his hands were squeezed behind his back. Again.

The man behind him tugged on the tie and forced Benji to walk toward one of the ATVs, then pushed him onto the seat facing forward. There was a graphite handle welded to the back of the seat that the man attached something to, and also to Benji's wrists.

"If you jump off I drag you," the man told Benji. "And I ain't stopping until we're there."

Benji did not outwardly react, but he completely understood. And he knew the man was serious—there was no doubt left in the tone of his voice and the delivery of his message. There were no games to be played, not this time, no way to escape. Whatever happened next was out of Benji's hands.

The man sat in front of Benji and the ATV rumbled to a start. Then one by one, each driver revved their ATV's engine and sped off back toward the clearing, back toward where they came from. And there was nothing Benji, or anyone else, could do to stop them.

# CHAPTER TWENTY-EIGHT

*About one year ago.* Everything changed for Sheila, finally for good, on a Monday. What she remembered about that day was that it began as any other day might. Ordinary. She woke up early and took a walk, then went back to her apartment and showered before heading to work. By then, she had made her way to Cedar Rapids, Iowa, and was bagging groceries at a supermarket by day. By night, she was a promiscuous clubgoer who enjoyed a little gin and dancing like nobody was watching. And for the most part nobody was, until they were. An infatuated lust began with a woman named Cheyenne, and what she learned helped her put her plan into overdrive. But that was a different story.

What happened on that seemingly ordinary Monday was anything but ordinary. On her way to work, her phone pinged with a new alert. Not unusual. So much so, she did not even bother looking at it until she arrived to the supermarket. When she did, she opened the alert, an email, and read the message.

The email landed in her fictitious email account, the one she used to communicate with Minka's school as her mother. All the email had was numbers and one symbol. Two strings of them. The first string could have been anything. Sheila sat down and unscrambled the numbers in the first string using the same information in the decoder she sent to Minka. The results meant nothing. After a few minutes of racking her brain trying to figure out what she was missing, it all clicked. The symbol was a plus sign, and it was directly in front of two numbers by themselves—a four and a six.

+46.

Sweden's country code.

It was a phone number.

Using the decoder a second time, Sheila unscrambled the second string of numbers, which was much shorter—only five numbers. When she did, she dropped her phone on the floor. It landed on its back, thankfully, and not the screen, because the message contained information she could not lose. The second string of words spelled her sister's name.

Minka.

The phone number was Minka's.

During her shift, Sheila mindlessly bagged customers' groceries, paying no mind to the repetitive beeping of the barcode scanner, and thought of Minka. She was high with anticipation about what this meant. Minka had her own phone now, which meant they could communicate privately. Sheila's plan might actually work.

On her lunch break, Sheila screenshotted the email and wrote it down, double-checked and triple-checked, then proceeded to permanently close the email account. After her shift, she hurried to the nearest mobile phone store and purchased a disposable one with an international calling card, and she texted the number from the email.

It took a few painstakingly long hours, but a response came back. It had been the middle of the night in Sweden when Sheila texted. Minka responded in the early morning hours while she was getting ready for school. When asked when the best time to call was, and Minka told Sheila to give her thirty minutes—that way, she would be walking to school and have privacy.

They were the longest thirty minutes of Sheila's life.

She was so nervous she nearly threw up. She even went into the bathroom at one point, just in case, but fought it off. Sweat poured off her as if she had just gotten out of the shower.

What would she say to Minka? After so many one-way messages that consisted of backstory and all the bad things, the realization hit her that she knew nothing about Minka. Not what she looked like or what her voice sounded like or what her interests were. The last time they spoke, Minka was a little kid who had a limited vocabulary and an abundance of saliva. Sheila could have, in theory, walked past Minka on the street one day and not know who she was. What if they had nothing in common? The age gap between them was wide. What if it was too far to bridge? How weird was it that she was risking everything, her life, to save a sister she knew absolutely nothing about? The more Sheila thought and overthought about it, the worse she felt.

Thirty minutes came. Finally. Sheila's heart pounded and her hands shook as she tried to swipe to dial the number. Twice she had to restart as her fingers pushed buttons other than the ones she wanted because of the trembling. She stopped, paused, and took a deep breath. She told herself she was being ridiculous. Then she tried again.

The call connected and the phone rang once, twice, thrice. Then someone answered it.

"Hello?" said the voice—a sweet but grown up, almost adultlike voice.

Tears immediately welled in Sheila's eyes. "Minka? It's Sheila."

Minka did not respond right away. And just when Sheila was about to repeat what she said, Minka finally did. "It's really you?"

Overwhelming joy engulfed her. The welled tears came pouring out. She felt the mascara smudge on her face, but she did not care, not at all. "It's really me."

They were giddy like two little girls after that. Not much speaking happened, mostly laughing.

"I need to go now," Minka said. "I'm at school."

"Yes, of course." Sheila remembered the walk; it was not very far. Even so, she was disappointed their conversation was already over.

"When can we talk again?" Minka asked.

"Tomorrow?"

"Yes!"

"Same time? I'll call you."

"Okay. Well, bye."

"Goodbye, Minka."

They hung up.

Sheila practically floated away.

·　·　·　·　·

They spoke on the phone for the few minutes it took Minka to walk to school every weekday, as often as they could. Excluding holidays or Sheila's work schedule or if it was too cold or rainy for Minka to walk and was driven in. By the second month, after they had run out of the basics to cover—Minka's favorite color was purple, Sheila's fuchsia; Minka liked to draw, Sheila used to too, back when she had free time; Minka made good marks in school, just like Sheila had—Sheila knew she had to move things along before they were found out. It would not take long before their father began asking questions about who Minka was talking to all the time; the number would be right on the phone bill. Which was exactly why Sheila used a burner phone with an area code far away from where she was, so her location could not be traced.

"Have you started making drop-offs for dad yet?" Sheila asked her with as much tenderness as should could muster.

"Yes. Two years ago I think."

When she was eleven, just like Sheila.

"I'm sorry."

Minka did not respond.

"We don't have to talk about it today if you don't want, but we need to talk about it."

"I know. It's okay."

"The men, have they started . . . you know?"

But did she know? Minka was only thirteen. Did she know about those things yet?

"One tried to touch me one time, if that's what you mean. But I kicked him in the shin and ran out."

This saddened Sheila. She felt as if she was too late. "Hang in there, okay? I have a plan to get you out of there. I just need a little more time."

"Okay. Oh, um, I have to go now."

"Go, go. I understand."

"Oh, and Sheila?"

"Yeah?"

"I love you."

She stopped. She had been pacing in her apartment, anxious about the conversation that needed to be had. Her heart fluttered. "And I love you, Minka. So, so, so much. I hope you know that."

"Yeah. Okay, I have to go now. Bye."

"Bye."

The very next day, she finished filling out the paperwork that had been on her kitchen table for weeks and delivered it. She had all the motivation she needed now. Through her immigration attorney, she had officially become a United States citizen a few months prior. Now that she was, she figured she should get her driver's license in case she ever needed it.

She waited in a long line at the DMV for hours on her day off until it was her turn to take the test, which she passed without any incorrect answers. After that, she drove around a borrowed car with an awkward man who held a clipboard and took notes.

"Take a left here," he said. Then: "Take a right here."

After a half hour of that, he handed her a sheet of paper that indicated she passed and congratulated her. After, she went back inside and stood in line for a while longer, then handed over the papers and smiled for the camera. All the while knowing doing so would put her name in a registry—using her birth name, Sheila Backe, not one of her aliases—and make her easier to track down. Which was why she had been holding out for as long as possible, until she knew for sure she was ready to move forward.

Which she was now.

Especially since that other thing with her friend Cheyenne was officially a go now too—the thing, the event, that truly changed everything that was to follow.

# CHAPTER TWENTY-NINE

*Present day.* The first bit of good news that Randolph received in what felt like forever was that all four of them arrived safely—he, Sheila, Benji, and Minka. Unless he counted the blisters forming on his palms and wrists from all the chafing, which he did not, he was none the worse for the wear. The others all seemed to be okay too.

The men on the ATVs did not say much of anything when they all pulled up in an empty field and killed the engines. Their weapons seemed to do most of the talking for them. While Randolph could not see their faces well based on the angles they stood, the man who drove Sheila was different. He stood in front of them all with his finger resting on the trigger as if it were stuck there permanently. His eyes bored into Sheila like he wanted to undress or execute her or both, the order of which unclear.

Sweat droplets trickled down Randolph's forehead. The unknown about where they were, what was happening, and who these men were was one thing, but add in the sweltering heat and the wide-open sky doing nothing to help, and he was roasting. He felt completely drained, exhausted beyond belief, between the frantic run to safety and now this—and he was running out of fight.

"Would now be a good time to ask what we're waiting for?" Benji said aloud, shockingly and maddeningly.

Why could he not just keep his mouth shut?

"Shut up," the alpha of the group said, the one in front. His gaze remained on Sheila.

No more than a few minutes after that, the action happened. It started with a distant whirring that quickly grew louder. It was a familiar sound but not something Randolph could place right away. Not until he saw it hovering above the tree line in the horizon. It was then the sound made perfect sense, even if its reason for being there was anything but.

A chopper raced toward them, its blade slicing through the sky with an ease that was easy for the engineer in Randolph to admire from afar. The machine's nose slanted downward, toward the earth, the rotor pushing it faster and faster. As it approached, the whirring became so deafeningly loud that Randolph's ears buzzed, and he had to squint and look away to avoid the windburn in his eyes. He struggled to remain standing as the gust from the helicopter pushed against his weakened body as it lowered itself toward the ground.

Even as the skids touched down and the bald-headed men lowered their weapons, Randolph still sensed the danger everywhere around him. The chopper door opened but no one stepped out, which the men with the rifles seemed to take as a cue. Before he had time to process what was happening or formulate a hypothesis, he stumbled forward. The man behind him started pushing him.

"What's going on?" Randolph asked him, not expecting a response and not getting one.

He stumbled forward again. And again. Toward the helicopter.

In his periphery, he saw the same thing happening to Benji—a man behind him and shoving him forward, Benji staggering with each step.

The girls, however, were not.

"Hey! What's going on?" Randolph said again, more forcefully this time. "Answer me, damn it!"

But the man behind him did not. Neither did any of the other men.

A shot of adrenaline kicked in.

"Wait!" Randolph shouted over the obnoxiously loud whirring of the blades. He could not even hear himself think.

He stepped forward and planted his heels into the dirt, then spun with all his might until he faced the gunman. The man did not react right away, but his shoulders were wide and strong enough to stop Randolph in his tracks as he tried to run back toward where they just were.

"Hey!" the man shouted as his arms opened and wrapped themselves around Randolph's.

Lots of voices began shouting.

Over the man's shoulder, Randolph spotted Sheila. Her mouth was agape and her eyes wide. He saw the back of a man in front of her now, seemingly holding her back just like the man in front of Randolph was doing to him.

"Sheila!" Randolph yelled out to her even though he knew it was no use. "Sheila!"

"No!" she shouted back, then something else he could not hear amid the chaos.

"Where are you taking me?" Randolph shouted again to anyone and everyone. "Sheila!"

Then just like that, the man in front of him lifted him up and began walking toward the helicopter as if he were a child. Sheila's legs flailed as someone did the same to her, just in the opposite direction. Randolph screamed until his lungs burned, even as

Sheila's voice got farther away and she disappeared into a shadow, silhouetted into blackness.

Randolph was tossed and he fell backward onto a hard floor. Before he even had time to sit up, a door closed and latched, and the helicopter lifted. He pushed onto his knees, smacked into Benji, who was already inside, and peered through the glass. Sheila was nowhere to been seen below. Minka was being forced to walk in the same direction Sheila had disappeared to.

"Noooo!" Randolph shrieked as the chopper picked up speed and flew away, leaving Sheila and Minka behind.

•   •   •   •   •

He had no inclination as to how much time passed until they touched ground again. Emptiness filled his mind—and heart. Sheila was gone.

Things were different when they landed. Much different. It was impossible not to sense it. The pilot and his copilot removed their headsets and shook hands, then slid out of the cockpit. After, the rear doors unlatched and slid open. Randolph looked down at the pilot, seeing his own sad reflection in the man's aviator sunglasses.

Without a word, the pilot retrieved a multitool from his belt and showed Randolph a pair of scissors. Randolph turned his shoulders and let the man cut him free while the same thing happened to Benji next to him. Once he was free, he turned back and faced the pilot, who offered a helping hand. Randolph took it without a second thought and stepped out of the helicopter. Benji joined him in the front.

"Gentlemen, come with us," the pilot with the cool shades said.

Randolph glanced in Benji's direction and saw no hesitation, so he went along. Whatever. He no longer cared.

They were on a roof. Of what, he could not tell. Around them were other roofs, some with greenery, others with nothing but ventilation systems sticking out the top. He heard an airplane in the distance.

The two pilots led them, without force, to a doorway on the far end of the rooftop. The copilot knocked twice with the side of his hand, and the door popped open. He fist bumped the man on the other side.

"This is as far as we go," the pilot said, crossing his arms behind his back.

"Where are we going?" Benji asked.

"Monty will take it from here."

The pilot and copilot turned and walked away, back toward their chopper.

"Are you Monty?" Benji asked the man holding the door open. A striped, yellow safety vest stretched against his stomach.

"This way, fellas," presumably Monty said.

Randolph followed Benji into the doorway.

The door closed behind them and Monty walked in front, leading them down a set of stairs and a long hallway, then another. They took a left then a right, descended another set of stairs, and took another right. Then finally, they reached another unmarked door.

Monty rested a forearm against the push bar and faced them. Randolph noted the beads of sweat on his forehead and was glad he was not the only one struggling with all the stairs. He figured Monty was around thirty.

"Tell them your names and you'll be all set," Monty said. "Any questions?"

"Uh, yeah," Benji answered. "What the hell is—"

"No? Good." Monty threw his weight against the bar and the door pushed open. He stood aside and let them pass. Monty would not look at Randolph as he passed him, which was what it was. He did not want to get involved in whatever was going on, which Randolph understood. The man had a job to do, and that was that. Maybe he had a family at home. Maybe he did not. Maybe he was one of them, whoever they were, despite having a full head of hair. It did not matter. Nothing mattered anymore.

The door closed behind them.

They stepped out into an airport terminal. People hurried around them. A lady dropped her purse and screeched, then gathered everything up so quickly and started running that it was like it never happened at all.

"There?" Benji said, pointing at the nearest gate that had a woman dressed like an employee might.

"Who knows?"

Benji went there. Randolph followed. A group of passengers waited in the seating area. One man read a hardcover book without the jacket. Another had his head back and his mouth open and could have been asleep. They walked right up to the woman at the lectern.

"Hello," the woman said with a welcoming smile. "May I help you?"

Benji looked at Randolph for approval, got none, and turned back to the woman. "We, um, we were told to give you or someone our names."

A blank expression swept across the woman's face.

"By Monty," Benji added. "It was Monty who said that."

"Your names?"

Randolph was not sure if it was a question or an invitation, but Benji took it as the latter. He gave the woman his name, then Randolph did too.

The woman looked down at something for a long few seconds, then looked back up. "Yes, I see you here. Okay, come with me."

Benji shrugged at Randolph, and they both blindly followed her.

The woman turned and approached the gate door, which she opened. Down the tunnel they went. At the end, the woman told them to wait where they were while she went ahead and spoke with one of the flight attendants. What about, who knew?

No more than two or three minutes later, the woman returned. She said, "Go ahead. Eliza will show you the way." Then she walked off, back toward where they came from.

Eliza was the flight attendant. She smiled a bubbly smile and greeted them, then escorted them to their seats—which, it turned out, were not ordinary seats. They were private seats. Loungers.

"Are we in first class?" Benji asked, though Randolph was thinking it too.

"Yes, Sir," Eliza said. "I hope you enjoy your accommodations. Is there anything I can get you while we wait for the other passengers to board?"

Benji looked at Randolph once again, but Randolph was not in the mood to engage with him.

"Vodka soda?" Benji said.

"Of course." Eliza looked at Randolph now. "And for you, Sir?"

"I'll take a scotch," Randolph added. "But you better make it a double."

# CHAPTER THIRTY

*Present day.* Flying first class made even long flights tolerable. And the flight—or, multiple flights, as it were—was quite long. So long, Benji stopped caring about how long it was. He simply lounged.

He felt a major sense of relief when the plane landed and he learned where he was—back in the United States. He had been for a while actually, having changed planes in Hawaii and passed through its airspace, but the continental United States was different. More permanent.

And damn, it was good to be home.

Regretfully, he had been unable to say goodbye to Randolph when they landed. They caught up in the air, but there was not much else to say that had not already been said. Neither one of them had any clue about what they were doing back in the United States or how, and who those men were in Palau. Understandably so, Randolph shut down when it came to talking about Sheila. Benji did not press. Now, Randolph was off to do his own thing, and Benji was off to do his. Although he really had no idea where he was going to go.

Now that he knew he would not be getting any money from Gary—which he had a feeling would happen all along because, why not?—he needed a new plan if he wanted to get to Fiji to see Justice.

*Justice.*

He sent her a heart emoji when she was on his mind, then pocketed his phone. He was inside an airport. He walked with the crowd. All the information he had been given from the airline was that there would be two men waiting for him when he landed. He was not told who they were or what they wanted, or what they looked like. All he was told was that he would know them when he saw them.

Helpful, right?

Not quite.

Despite the infuriation of the unknown that could have tormented him, Benji was surprisingly calm. With Gary now out of the picture, so it seemed, it felt like a weight was lifted. Whatever was to happen next could in no way be as bad as what Gary had put him through.

Right?

Wrong.

He knew it immediately.

The two men stood out like sore thumbs. While everyone around them hurriedly dragged luggage and carried boarding passes and talked on mobile phones, or to each other, these men stood like pricks. They both wore sunglasses—yes inside, hence why they were pricks—and all black clothing. From the slacks to the blazers to the undershirt, neckties, and shoes, all of which made their pale faces stand out even more than they already did. The men were nearly the same height and both stood with their arms dangling by their sides, unmoving as if they were royal guards.

Once Benji saw them he could not unsee them. Everyone who passed in front of them blurred, leaving the men in perfect clarity in his line of sight. A small lump formed in his throat as he walked toward them, crossing between foot traffic going in both directions.

Up close, the men were massive. Well over six feet tall and deliberately fit as a way of intimidation, he figured. Benji felt, and surely looked, like a twig beside them.

"Are you guys, by chance, waiting for someone?" Benji asked.

Predictably, they did not respond.

"Benji, perhaps?"

One of the giants craned his neck down at Benji.

"I'm Benji."

Both men turned on a dime and indicated for him to follow them. He did what was requested of him as the men started walking. Benji followed them into a door painted the same color as the wall not far from where they were. If the man in the front had not reached forward and pushed the door open, Benji would not have known it was there. It made him wonder what other secrets airports kept.

On the other side of the door was a room with padded walls, a rectangular table, and one chair. No windows. No air vents. And most disturbingly, no cameras in the corners of the ceiling. Whatever happened in this room stayed in this room.

The lump in Benji's throat grew a little larger.

One of the big men walked around the table and pulled the chair out. He motioned for Benji to sit. He did. Then the big man walked back around the table and joined the other big man. They both, finally, took off their sunglasses.

"Should we do introductions?" Benji asked, trying to lighten the mood.

"We know who you are," one of the men said.

Benji nodded. He folded his hands on the table and twirled his thumbs. Waited.

Without further prompting, both men walked toward him, each of them slapping something on the table. Benji leaped back in surprise. Once he regained his composure, he peered at the table to what the men were showing him.

"Whoa, whoa, whoa!" he said, bewildered. "You're feds? I don't know what you think I did, but I think you have me mixed up with someone else."

"Violation of your terms of release," one of the men said. "Cybercrimes. Hacking. All federal crimes."

Both men flipped closed their badges.

"Luckily for you," the same man went on, "we're feeling generous today. I'm Agent Weasley. This is Agent Jax. You can call me Agent Weasley. Not Weasley, not Mister, not Mr. Weasley. Agent Weasley. Got it?"

"What about him?"

"Agent Jax," Agent Jax said.

"Not just Jax?" Benji asked.

"Do you think you're funny?" Agent Weasley asked. "Don't answer that."

Benji shifted. Having their names helped. Made them feel more relatable.

"You're a very lucky man, you know?" Agent Weasley said.

"Doesn't feel that way."

"Do you know who those men were that captured you in Palau?"

He did, but he thought it might be better to play dumb. He shook his head.

"You ever heard of Crips?"

"A little."

Agent Weasley went on to give Benji a summary of everything he already knew about the Crips—who they were, what they did, what their motivations were. Benji listened and nodded as if hearing it for the first time.

"They're bad dudes," Agent Weasley said. "You should be dead right now."

Comforting.

"But I'm not."

"No," Agent Weasley said. "No, you're not. Consider yourself fortunate that you were of no use to them. They got what they wanted."

Sheila.

"Why am I here?"

"We were hoping you could tell us that."

Benji was confused. "I don't know what you mean."

"What can you tell us about Gary O'Reilly?"

He almost laughed. "This is about Gary?"

"How do you know him?"

Benji thought long and hard about his answer. Where did it all begin? He was not even sure where to start. How much did they know about everything that happened in Iowa? To tell them how he knew Gary meant rehashing all that—the hacking, the pipe bomb, Patricia, then Fiji and Palau. Rehashing all that meant revealing more crimes than he cared to admit he was guilty of. Admitting to all that also meant losing any leverage he may have, if such a thing existed, and giving away the only bargaining chip he had: his life.

"I don't think I want to answer that," Benji said. That was his right, he knew.

The agents looked at one another as if surprised.

"Are you refusing to answer our questions?" Agent Weasley asked.

Was he?

"I didn't say that. I just said I didn't want to answer that question."

"That's your right to do that, absolutely. But if you don't give us information, we can't help you. And if we can't help you, that means we'll have no choice but to send you back where you came from. I'm not an expert, but I do believe you're looking at an additional five years, at least, for leaving the county, per the terms of your release. Is that right, Agent Jax?"

"That's right."

"Are you willing to give up five more years of your twenties behind bars, Benjamin Griffin?"

Was he?

*Justice.*

"What kind of deal are we talking about?" Benji asked.

"A good deal," Agent Weasley responded. "A very, very good deal. We're offering you your life back."

That got Benji's attention. He sprung upright. "Are you talking about a clean slate?"

"You catch on quick."

"Just for telling you what I know about Gary O'Reilly?"

"That's right."

It was a no-brainer.

"Hell yes, I'm in. I'll tell you every damn thing there is to know about the guy. What do you want to know first?"

Agent Weasley turned to Agent Jax and smiled, then he turned back to Benji. "You want some water or something? Maybe some chips or a bag of pretzels? Anything?"

"I just want to get the hell out of here."

"Well, great. Let's get to it."

"I just have one request first."

Agent Weasley's face fell slightly. "Which is?"

"The last deal I made was bullshit. Worthless. Clearly, because I'm here. This time, I want to make sure it's done right."

Agent Weasley said nothing.

"I want a lawyer."

# CHAPTER THIRTY-ONE

*Less than one year ago.* While Sheila had sworn off men romantically—Liam, remember?—that did not mean she could not be friends with them. Which was what happened when she met a young guy by chance one day. She was walking into the bank to deposit her paycheck when, out of nowhere, someone walked right into her. The purse in her hand went flying. It had been zipped and did not spill, but she still gasped and quickly bent down as if it had.

The guy did the same thing. Their eyes locked.

His name was Benji.

Benji was shy at first, hesitant to respond to her banter—or did not know how to—but came out of his shell before long and invited her to join him for coffee the next day. Just as friends, so he could apologize for crashing into her. She accepted. Why not?

She and Benji exchanged numbers and texted here and there afterward, but their relationship was nothing serious. There was no romantic spark between them. She thought it was nice to have a friend.

Which was why she felt terrible about what would happen next.

Her other new friend, Cheyenne, had fallen for her. Hard. Sheila knew it. And while she hated herself for lying about it— that she had the same feelings for Cheyenne—she was quick to forgive herself too. It was all about the end goal.

Minka.

Vulnerability was a powerful experience. Sheila recognized it in Cheyenne, and in Benji, who started intimately opening up to her too, and took advantage of it—of them. They were both weak-willed for different reasons—Benji for his loneliness and lack of connection with his family; Cheyenne for her pure, sickening hatred of her husband whom she spoke terribly of. Cheyenne was in the middle of a nasty divorce and was going to be screwed financially. And after all the time she had committed to her husband—or as she called him, the dickless coward—she felt she was due more. She thought she deserved more for wasting most of her adult life being unsatisfied.

And the only way to get more was to get all of it, if her husband was dead before the divorce was final because they had a prenuptial agreement in place that stripped her of her rights.

Sheila was nearly out of savings. Her job at the supermarket paid enough to pay her bills, but nothing else. Some months, depending on how many shifts she had, she was a little short and had to dip into that dwindling savings account. Which pushed her even further away from Minka. She needed a lot of money if this was going to happen, and she needed it fast.

Cheyenne's husband, and therefore Cheyenne, had money. Lots of it. Getting her hands on that money would prove to be complicated.

Sheila arranged for Cheyenne and Benji to meet, and the rest was history. Cheyenne threw some money at him, Benji built a bomb, and Sheila lingered in the shadows—playing forever lover to both Cheyenne and Benji, while actually planning on being neither; it was all about Minka, after all. Always.

Everything went wrong in the execution. Sheila was distracted by Cheyenne's husband's charm and missed the critical transfer, and the next thing she knew, everything backfired. Instead of Cheyenne collecting on all the marital assets and running away to Fiji with Sheila, her husband survived. And he was the sweetest, kindest, most gentle man Sheila had ever met.

That was not part of the plan. He was supposed to be the cruel, robotic, soulless man Cheyenne had described. If he was that man, it would have made everything easy to justify; Sheila knew bad men, and it was about time they got what they deserved.

But Randolph was different.

Cheyenne had put a down payment on a condo in Fiji where she and Sheila would start over, together, as a couple. Except that would never happen. Sheila needed the place in Fiji as a shadow, just a place to help her cover her tracks and get Gary off her back. And just in case Patricia turned on her once she found out her true intentions, she might have sent whoever to Fiji to go after Sheila just like she had with her husband, and Sheila would not have been there.

Patricia had cashed out an old investment and transferred $150,000 to Sheila's personal account, which she used to put toward the condo. That way, it was Sheila—or one of her aliases, Guinevere Somalia—who would carry the property under her name so to not raise any red flags during Cheyenne's divorce; if Cheyenne did not own the property, it could not be included in the joint assets with her husband and sold.

None of that happened.

What Sheila really wanted to accomplish was to rescue Minka from Sweden. Once she got her cut from the death of Cheyenne's husband, Sheila was going to disappear again with the money and put her extraction plan into action. In each place she stayed across Europe, she rented a post office box. She had planned to mail a chunk of cash to each P.O. box that Minka could grab during each leg of her journey. Using the trail Sheila left on the postcards, Minka would follow Sheila's route to the boxes, collect the money, and continue on.

The sisters would meet up in Palau—Sheila's favorite place on earth, as she once told Randolph, although she had never been; it had been a clue for him, if he was smart enough to figure it out on his own—and start a new life with Cheyenne's money. After enough time had passed, Sheila would contact her immigration attorney and head back to the States. Where, as a citizen, her sister could be granted a green card too out of familial ties. By then, she had hoped either Gary would have given up completely or have forgotten about it and moved on to other cases. Or she could have fought back with the help of her immigration attorney, now that she had the available funds to do so.

What she had not planned for was him working for her father. Or falling completely, madly, head over heels in love with Randolph.

After that happened, she had no plan. She would have told him the truth about everything once she knew how he felt about her, and she almost did. More than once. But the right moment never struck, and before they had enough time for the right moment to present itself, Gary showed up in Utah and put the kibosh on it all.

Sheila had no choice but to take off, as much as it killed her to leave Randolph behind. She felt at home with Randolph's family, the family she longed for. But she also had a family back home she needed to take care of—Minka—and she had to get out. And she had to do it fast.

Instead of using an alias, Sheila used her real name and real passport to book a flight to Fiji. Gary would connect the dots between her flight and her alias owning the property in Fiji and figure out where she was going, except she was one step ahead of him. She never even left the airport. She arrived in Fiji and booked another flight back to the United States, this time using one of her aliases. So as far as Gary knew, she was in Fiji, and he would spend time looking for her there. Which he did.

Meanwhile, Sheila was under his nose the whole time, hiding out in a small Florida city. Meanwhile, Minka was making her way across Europe, collecting the cash Sheila mailed, and making her way toward her.

When she received the text message from Randolph one night asking the name of the town they stayed in when they were in Nebraska, she knew he was in trouble. She had been monitoring the situation from afar—though not really that far— so she already had a feeling something was not right. Something was off about the tone of his message. And when he asked if they could talk, in-person, he all but confirmed it. She swiped a taxi, met him at the bus station, and warned him. And thankfully, he listened and agreed to meet up later, and she told him everything.

Well, not quite everything.

That came later, once she convinced him to go with her. Two weeks on a cruise ship would give them time to reconnect—and would not give him a choice but to listen, since he would have nowhere to go. She could only plan so much ahead of time, so the rest was blind faith. He understood, or seemed to, and was on her side. That was the final confirmation she needed that he did, truly, feel about her the way she felt about him. That was all she needed to fight for him, whatever that meant. She would do whatever it took to be together. And that meant anything.

# CHAPTER THIRTY-TWO

*Present day.* There was only one place Randolph wanted to go after he safely landed home and gave an awkward goodbye to Benji, who seemed to want more. Randolph did not have much to give. He felt bad about it, sure, but he could barely muster up enough energy to support himself, never mind someone else. Secure your own mask first before you help someone else, so they say.

His heart ached. Having been torn from Sheila and filled with doubt, then realizing that what they had all along was actually meaningful and real, then reconciling. Only then to have it all stripped away from him again was just about all he could handle. Sleep failed him. His mind ran a thousand miles a minute when he closed his eyes, wondering where Sheila was and if she was okay and if he would ever see her again. And as much as he tried to avoid negative thoughts, the realist in him had to question whether she was alive at all.

He felt terrible. Emotionally drained and empty. Overcome with physical exhaustion. Mentally checked out. What he needed right now was family.

The sign welcoming him to Green River, Utah, did not have the same effect on him as it had in the past. Once he would have been joyous and filled with love and anticipation, but in his current state of mind all he felt was dread. It was a mixed bag of emotions. On one hand, he knew he had to reconcile with Bruce—he wanted to—after their blowout the last time Randolph was in Utah. Especially with the new baby coming into the world very soon. Randolph could not remember exactly how many weeks pregnant Janet was at the point, although he was all but certain she was in the ninth month. Despite that, Randolph knew resolving his differences with Bruce would not be easy, and he did not have much psychological wherewithal to properly handle it right now.

But he had no choice. Frankly, he had nowhere else to go. The house in Iowa had been sold. Before, his plan had been to crash on Bruce's sofa for a while until he settled in and found a small place of his own nearby. That way, Randolph would be around to help with the new baby or to take Maxwell off his parents' hands for a few hours while they got some much-needed rest or time to bond with the new family member. At the time it sounded like a solid plan, a best of both worlds situation, but that was not how it happened. Gary and Benji and Sheila happened all over again, then Patricia, and Randolph's entire world spun out of control. And now he was left to try to pick up the pieces left in the wake of the storm.

As the cab pulled into Bruce's neighborhood, Randolph felt a twisting in his gut. He had nothing—no bag, no change of clothes—including a clue about what he might say to his only son if he actually opened the door. There were so many things to say, yet so little too. He had explained his relationship with Sheila to Bruce before, not that he needed to. As for what happened most recently, why Randolph had to up and leave again out of the blue, that would take more finessing.

Randolph paid the cab driver from the few bucks he had left in his wallet and got out on the street. Before he had time to ask him if he would stick around for a minute or two, just in case Bruce slammed the door in Randolph's face, the driver pulled away and disappeared around the bend.

It was shortly after dawn. The neighborhood was hushed aside from the singing robins. A power walking woman passed him on the opposite side of the street without acknowledgement. A few houses had exterior lights on, but most did not. Randolph's quads pounded as he climbed up the driveway, his chest right along with them. His eyelids felt like they weighed a hundred pounds each.

Bruce's porch looked to be about a million yards away through Randolph's barely functional tunnel of vision. Amazingly, Randolph made impeccable time and the million quickly turned into a thousand, then a hundred, then about two steps away. He dropped a hand on the smooth wood of the railing and grabbed it, then used its strength to help give him some of his own. He pulled himself up, one slow, painstaking step at a time.

The front door squeaked open. Through his fog, Randolph only saw darkness and the silhouette of a featureless person. The door squeaked again as it closed, then smacked against the frame once with a thud.

"What are you doing here?" It was his son's voice. Bruce.

"I wanted to make sure you got my last message," Randolph said, smiling.

The joke fell flat. Bruce did not laugh.

"Seriously, Dad. You can't keep showing up here without calling first. I know you're going through some stuff right now but—"

It was at that point that Randolph lost it. Any façade of toughness he had left crumbled into bits on his son's porch. All the pent up emotion—the sadness and the fear and the anger and the despair—poured out of him. It all came out in the form of thick, sopping tears that drenched his cheeks and sucked out what little energy remained. Randolph felt his muscles weaken. His knees shook as his vision blurred. His grip strength weakened as his fingers struggled to maintain their grasp on the railing.

He heard nothing as his knees buckled and the weight of his world came crashing down onto Bruce's porch. Then everything went black.

·    ·    ·    ·    ·

Randolph was awoken by the compress of a cool cloth on his forehead, along with the gentlest, most soothing humming he had ever heard. The muscles in the back of his head were tense with exhaustion, but he felt a strange sense of calm.

He opened his eyes and saw the bright, smiling face of Janet hovering above him, mothering him like her instincts often told her she should.

"Hi," she said, her smile as warming as ever. "Feeling better?"

Randolph grunted and slid his arms underneath his torso to push himself upward. "Water?"

Unsurprisingly, Janet already had a glass ready. She grabbed it from the table next to her and handed it to him. He sat up fully and guzzled it.

"Thank you," he said. Then he wiped his lips with the side of his hand.

She took the now empty glass and set it back down beside her.

He looked at his daughter-in-law now. Studied her. Relief flooded through him when he saw her still pregnant belly—which meant he had not missed the birth; there was still time. Although she had to have been miserable, she had him fooled. Janet glowed with the joy of a woman born to be a mother. She cradled and rubbed her womb as if it were the most delicate piece of machinery known to mankind. She was an absolute natural.

"Has anyone ever told you you're amazing?" he asked her.

While it did not seem possible, her smile grew even wider. "Right back at you."

He smiled now too. He was so happy Bruce found a woman like Janet—or Janet, specifically. "Where's Bruce?"

"Went for a walk around the neighborhood with Max."

"Is he angry?"

"He'll be fine." She smiled at him again, as if a smile helped to soften the blow of the bad news she would not deliver.

Which it kind of did.

"What day is it?"

"Saturday."

"What year?"

Janet's expression changed. Worry. She straightened.

"I'm just kidding."

She pressed a hand to her chest and laughed. "Not funny," she joked. "A pregnant woman shouldn't be stressed out, you know."

He smiled at her. "You're right, I'm sorry. How are you feeling, by the way?"

"I'm good. Well, actually, I'm miserable"—she laughed—"but that's okay. Only a couple more weeks."

"I'm glad I'm here."

"I'm glad you're here too. Max will be thrilled to see his Grandpop."

Just then, a squeak rang through the house, followed by some thumping and a muffled child's voice.

"Speaking of," Janet said. "Here"—she extended her hand toward Randolph—"let me help you up."

"You're the pregnant one here, not me." Randolph drove his palms into the mattress—he was on Bruce and Janet's bed, he now realized—and pushed himself up. Everything hurt when he stood, but he ignored the discomfort. He faced Janet and reached his hand out to her. She smiled and took it, and he pulled her to her feet.

"Mummy!"

Randolph turned and saw Maxwell loping toward his mother with extended arms and a grin just as wide as hers.

"Hi, baby!" she said to him, somehow managing to crouch down and scoop him up without toppling over.

They shared a long embrace while Janet swung him back and forth, Maxwell's legs dangling.

"Do you see who's here?" Janet asked her boy. She turned so her back was to Randolph, so Maxwell faced him.

Randolph did not know what to do. The last time he saw Maxwell, he felt like he disappointed him by leaving so soon without saying goodbye. If Maxwell was anything like his mother, maybe Randolph might have the chance to redeem himself.

"Grandpop," Maxwell said bashfully.

"Hi, Maxwell," Randolph said as he waved with his fingers only.

"Grandpop!"

Randolph lit up. Then the floor creaked and he faced the doorway, and in walked Bruce.

"Okay, Dad," Bruce said, followed by a big sigh. His hair was disheveled but he looked otherwise centered, as if a little fresh air helped to cleanse him. "Let's go talk."

And talk they would.

# CHAPTER THIRTY-THREE

*Present day.* Benji enjoyed a few snacks and a room temperature bottle of water on the government's dime. None of them were particularly satiating, but the thought of where they came from made them taste just a bit better. He very much enjoyed having someone work for him for a change, or so it felt.

He felt like he was in a position of power, maybe—no, definitely—for the first time in his life. The agents wanted something he had, and it was entirely up to him how much information he shared—or did not share. How would they even know if he was holding back? They would not. He knew that, and he knew they must have been aware of that too. Which meant he was in complete control.

An attorney was on the way, he was told, sit tight. He did. The agents left him alone in the padded room. He did not mind. He enjoyed some salty pretzels. He felt like kicking off his shoes and putting his feet on the table but thought better of it.

An hour later, the nearly invisible door popped open and in walked the two giant men. Lingering behind was a much smaller man—and a bit dorky, Benji thought, with his rounded glasses and thinning hair and stuffy suit. The dork cradled a briefcase under his arm and walked right toward Benji without a word. He tossed his briefcase on the table, unhinged it, and pulled out a notepad and a pen.

"Chair?" the dorky man asked, though it was more of a demand.

Agent Jax left the room in a hurry as if he understood that too. Nobody spoke. The dork squared his pad on the table top and latched his briefcase. Agent Jax returned a few moments later with a folding chair. He walked around the table, unfolded said chair, and departed the room again. He returned with two more identical chairs and set them up where Agent Weasley stood. All three previously seatless men now sat.

"All right, gentlemen," the dork began, "this is how this is going to work. You may ask your questions now, and my client may answer with my permission. If I don't give him permission, you won't ask the question again. Understand?"

Both agents nodded.

"Good."

By now, Benji assumed the dorky man was the attorney they had all been waiting for. "Are you my—"

"Let's not talk," the presumed dorky attorney said without looking at Benji. "The only time you need to speak is in response to a question these men ask you—but only if I give you permission. Otherwise, no talking."

That was that.

Despite the man's look, he carried himself with an irrefutably alpha presence that was difficult to understand but easy to see and feel. It seemed the agents respected him too, which had to have meant something. Benji was happy to have him on his side, despite him not being the warmest person he had ever met.

Agent Weasley cleared his throat and said, "Gary O'Reilly. How do you know him?"

Benji glanced at the nameless attorney, who nodded. Then Benji gave him the rundown—the abbreviated version. Their first meeting was when he and Cheyenne—or Patricia, he later learned—were at the airport. Gary walked up to Benji and demanded he come with him, though he would not say why. Benji begrudgingly obliged, then was questioned about why he had hacked into the security tapes from the security system in the supermarket that exploded. Despite an initial effort to hold back, Gary presented him with footage of the supermarket— specifically with Shay, or Sheila's, face on it. That was where the story ended.

"That's it?" Agent Weasley asked once Benji finished. "What happened after that?"

Benji glanced at the attorney again, who nodded.

"Actually, never mind," Agent Weasley said, to Benji's initial delight. "We know what happened after that. It's all right here in this file." He motioned to the manila folder on the table in front of him.

"Why'd you ask if you already know?" Benji asked, annoyed.

"First of all, I'll be the one asking the questions. Secondly, as a show of good faith, I'll answer your question. I asked because I wanted to test your honesty. If you lie to us, no deal. We require one hundred percent honesty from you if we're to move forward."

"Actually, I'll be the one deciding the terms of the deal," the attorney said.

"All due respect, but—"

Agent Jax fake coughed into his fist, stopping Agent Weasley before he could finish his thought.

"That's a conversation for another time," said Agent Weasley. "Let's get back to the business at hand, shall we?"

Nobody answered.

"Good. Benji—can I call you Benji? I know your mother named you Benjamin, and I also know your father—"

"Benji's fine," Benji said. The early stages of his blood boiling began.

Agent Weasley smirked an evil smirk at him.

"Next question," the attorney said.

Agent Weasley wiped the smirk off his face. "I know that Gary O'Reilly had you released under his observation. The record shows you were assisting on a special assignment. But it also says you weren't supposed to leave the county and that you were to return to jail within ten days, once the special assignment was complete."

"I was never told that. I knew about the county, but Gary said he'd take care of it. I thought I was out permanently."

"I see." Agent Weasley pulled a sheet of paper from the folder and slid it toward Benji. "Have you seen this document before?"

It looked like the one he signed in jail, to get out. "I'm not sure."

Agent Weasley pointed to the bottom of the page. "Is this your signature?"

Benji studied it. "It looks like it, yes."

"Then according to this, you have seen this document, which are the terms of your release. It says here, in section one-A, that—and I quote—'The Subject'—that's you, you're the Subject—'will return to incarceration within ten days, regardless if the special assignment is completed.'" Agent Weasley looked up at Benji.

"Let me see that," the attorney said. He grabbed it and looked at it.

"I don't remember reading that. Gary told me—"

"Let me give you some free advice. Never, ever, trust a man like Gary at his word. And never sign a document without reading it first."

Benji felt defeated. Everything Gary had told him was a flat-out lie. Gary did not wipe the conviction clean. He never would have given Benji money because he knew Benji would go back to jail since he left the county—to a place Gary sent him! And while Benji was not sure what day it was anymore, it had most definitely been more than ten days since he was released.

"I know what you're thinking," Agent Weasley said. "Yes, we have a warrant for your arrest. Would you like to see it?"

Benji shook his head.

"I would," the attorney said.

Agent Jax retrieved another sheet of paper from the folder and handed it across the table.

"But as we've told you," Agent Weasley went on, "we're not concerned about that. You're a small-time criminal. Let's be honest, between you and me, I think a slap on the wrist will do. You're a young guy, I feel like you've learned your lesson to stay out of the hacking game. Am I right?"

Benji nodded.

"Your skills can be used for good, you know. You ever heard of government agencies hiring counterfeiters help identify other counterfeiters?"

Benji had. He nodded again.

"Well they do that with hackers too. If that interests you, we can put you in touch with the right people. Once we get what we want, of course."

The offer almost seemed too good to be true, but the attorney had no objections. For that, neither did Benji.

"So, now that we've established that," Agent Weasley said, "what we're really after are the big fish."

Gary was a big fish?

"We know you went to Fiji and that more than one dead body showed up after you got there."

"How do you . . . I had nothing to do with that!"

"We know that. We know just about everything, Benji. What we don't, we need you to fill in the gaps. So, why Fiji?"

Benji looked at the attorney again, who nodded.

"We were looking for Sheila."

"Sheila Backe?"

Benji nodded.

The two agents looked at one another, dumbfounded.

Agent Weasley turned back and said, "Why would Gary be looking for Sheila Backe?"

Now Benji was the one feeling confused. Was it not obvious? "Gary had boxes of files on her. Everything you could possibly imagine and some you probably couldn't. Or maybe you could, how the hell do I know?"

The agents shared another awkward look.

"He had this document on her. A color. Not actually a color, but you know what I mean? It was called a color. Blue something."

"A blue notice?" Agent Weasley asked.

"That was it."

The room fell silent briefly as if everyone was in deep thought.

Agent Weasley broke the silence with: "But why would Gary send civilians out there to look for her? I don't get that."

"He told us there was a financial incentive."

"To find her?"

"That's what he said."

Agent Weasley shifted as if uncomfortable. "That's not how INTERPOL works. Folks don't get . . . bonuses for doing their job."

"He said if we'd help, we'd get a cut of whatever he was making. Six eyes are better than two, I guess."

Agent Jax leaned in and whispered something in Agent Weasley's ear. He put a hand over his mouth so his lips could not be read.

"Are you sure?" Agent Weasley asked him.

Agent Jax nodded.

Agent Weasley turned back to Benji. "How much do you know about Sheila's father, Hector?"

"Nothing."

Which was mostly true. All he knew was what Minka and Sheila had talked about—that he was somehow connected to Gary, which Benji was still trying to figure out in his head.

"There was nothing about him in all those files you said Gary had on her?"

"None. I remembered wondering that when I looked through it, actually. All the information Gary had started when Sheila was sixteen. There was nothing before that."

Agent Weasley's face lit up. So did Agent Jax's.

"I think you've just given us the smoking gun we were looking for, Benji," Agent Weasley said.

He did? He did not even say anything.

"That's the missing piece right there. We'll need to check it out, but it all makes perfect sense now. Sometimes it's the most obvious answers that evade you the most. It was right in front of our faces the whole time!"

"I've got to be honest with you," Benji said. "I have no clue what you're talking about. Who's Sheila's dad? Who's Hector? And what does that have to do with anything?"

Agent Weasley went on to explain what was happening. Hector Backe, Sheila's father, traveled in well-known circles in Sweden—well-known by law enforcement. He was into drug dealing and smuggling, and was one of the kingpins in the cocaine trade in the region and beyond. He used his kids to transport the drugs as a way to shadow himself from capture. Law enforcement looked in one place, and he moved drugs in another. He lived modestly on the surface—no fancy cars, an ordinary-sized home, no lavish vacations—but it turned out, he was supremely wealthy. The truth about Hector was learned only recently, when he was arrested.

Benji knew this part—Minka had mentioned that their father was arrested a few days before she ran away. The link between him and Gary still did not make any sense.

But it was not just the money and the drugs that made Hector a kingpin. He was the top man in what was essentially the drug division of an organized crime group. He was known on the streets as King—for kingpin. And the group he was the leader of? The Crips.

Benji thought back to Fiji and Sheila's spray-painted condo.

*CRIP.*

*GNIK.*

King Crips.

"Okay," Benji said, processing. "Sheila's dad is King Crips and she used to run drugs for him. Got it. But what does that have to do with Gary? Sounds like an awful lot of work for INTERPOL to bust someone for selling drugs."

"No, no, no," Agent Weasley said, shaking his head. "You're missing the point. It's not about the drugs."

"It's not?"

"No. The drugs triggered the blue notice, okay? A blue notice is given out to someone wanted for questioning about a criminal investigation."

"So INTERPOL wants to talk to her about what happened when she was a kid?"

"Exactly."

"And . . . what? That's it?"

"No, that's not it. You also have to account for the money you said Gary was after. And like I said, INTERPOL doesn't give bonuses to people who execute their assigned duty."

"So where is the money coming from?" Although now, Benji saw where this was headed.

"Ah-ha! Exactly! That's the correct question. You're pretty slick, you know that? You catch on quick."

Benji did not know whether to thank him or roll his eyes.

"And based on our little chat here, I think we've connected all the dots. You've been a great help."

He still did not know what he actually said or did that helped, but he went with it.

"The money Gary mentioned, we presume, can only have come from one place."

"Which is?"

"None other than Mr. Backe himself." Agent Weasley folded his arms and smiled like a proud child might.

Benji let that sink in. That was the link; that was how Gary and Hector were working together. "So you're telling me that Sheila's dad was paying Gary to find Sheila?"

"That is what I'm telling you."

"And also that INTERPOL was looking for her to question her about what happened with her father when she was a kid?"

"Also yes."

"And Gary was working both sides of the fence?"

"Ding-ding-ding! What does he win? A new car!"

Benji turned to the attorney and said, "Are you writing that down?"

The dork glared at him.

"But seriously," Agent Weasley said, "We have more than enough to convict Gary now, thanks to you. Between all the dead bodies in his wake, unauthorized negotiations, and misusing INTERPOL technology, among a myriad of other things we don't need to get into, we've been watching him for a while. And now, with this new information, it's all but a lock that his reign is over."

Agent Weasley stood and held out his hand for Benji to shake, which he did after standing himself. Agent Jax then stood too, followed by the attorney.

"Thank you for your assistance in this matter," Agent Weasley said. "While the agency does its best to weed out the bad apples in the beginning, there's inevitably one or two that slip through the cracks. Now we've taken another one down, thanks in part to you."

Benji did not know what to say.

"If you're still interested in that job, we'll be more than happy to put a good word in. Isn't that right, Agent Jax?"

"That's right," Agent Jax said with a small smile.

"Gentlemen," the attorney said, "it sounds to me like my client has done everything you've asked. I think it's about time we draft up some language to get him out of here."

"I think you're right," Agent Weasley said.

"Hang tight," the attorney said to Benji. "You'll be a free man again in no time."

# CHAPTER THIRTY-FOUR

*Present day.* A couple of days had passed since the helicopter took off with the love of her life, against his will, inside. Her heart had still not recovered; it ached with a hurt so deep that all she wanted to do was lay down and sleep. Even as she knew she needed to try to be strong for Minka, the heartache of being torn away from Randolph again suffocated her from the inside out.

It took two men to pick Sheila up off the grass after the helicopter flew out of sight, and another to help carry her away. The men took her back into the mouth of the forest, back where the ATVs were hidden. She wailed but did not fight the men, though she did not help them either. She felt lifeless in their arms, completely empty inside. Randolph being taken was like a void in her soul that could never be replaced. Without him, she could not function.

One of the men had radioed to someone, then an off-road utility vehicle rumbled into the clearing a short while later. The three men carried Sheila's practically lifeless body toward it. She could not remember much aside from the hollow feeling inside as her limbs dangled, and how hard the bed of the off-roader felt against her back as they put her on it and let her go. She remembered sensing Minka near her, with her in the back of the off-roader. And even while Sheila knew she had to be stronger for Minka, to show her baby sister strength, she just did not have it in her; she was just barely hanging on herself.

The ride was choppy and nauseating as the tires hit and bounced out of holes in every direction. Just when she thought vomiting was a near certainty, the terrain would level out for a few minutes and her belly would settle, only to repeat the process many times over. Mother nature's form of humor, it seemed.

The off-roader pulled up to a wooden shack that was in remarkably good condition, as if it had been recently constructed. They were still in the woods. Black shingles lined the roof and had a noticeable seal to keep the outside out. A long brick-lined chimney popped out of the roof. No visible cracks. Thick logs stood tall as walls. Two massive stones made a short stairway into the structure.

Inside the shack was simplistic but functional. A set of bunkbeds against the far wall, each nicely made and with two pillows. An office-sized refrigerator shared a wall with a single-burner stove and a narrow stainless steel sink. Oak cabinets lined the walls above them. On the opposite wall, a toilet peeked out from behind a partition wall that folded in like an accordion. All that remained was a jute loveseat.

Sheila and Minka had not left the shack since arriving.

It was warm inside but not too hot, despite having only a single window. The door was locked from the outside. Men came and went, delivering plates of food and rolls of toilet paper, sometimes shampoo or hand soap. By the third morning, Sheila felt a semblance of strength trying to return. She woke up not needing to weep and feeling somewhat motivated to start formulating a plan on how to escape.

Minka was quiet throughout, had not said much. That was something Sheila felt guilty about; she felt like it was her fault. Minka, despite her bravery and courage, was just a kid, and Sheila had not been there for her in the least. As a sister, she failed her. But she would make it up to her. They had their whole lives together after this was over.

Which meant they had to get out.

The timing could not have been better for what happened next. Just as Sheila had begun to focus on the inside of the shack, paying attention to the corners where the walls met the ceiling and the framing of the door and window, looking for weak spots she could take advantage of, there was a sound outside. Sheila froze and put a finger to her lips to shush an already silent Minka, and she watched the door. Waited. Someone, or something, fumbled around with the door handle—either a man with a key or a bear with its paw.

Neither one seemed worse than the other.

It was a man. The door pushed open and the morning filled the interior of the shack with so much light, Sheila had to look away. Once her eyes adjusted and she could turn back, her gaze landed on the man. He was not one she recognized.

"Today's the day," the man said in an even tone.

"The day for what?" Sheila retorted.

"The day you two get out of here. Are you ready to leave?"

Sheila glanced at Minka to gauge her reaction. There was not much there. Resignation, maybe.

"Let's go," the man said. "You can eat on the way."

⁕⁕⁕

The man was right. A box of bagels awaited them in the back of an extended cab pickup truck. The man graciously helped both Sheila and Minka up. Even the designated step was a long stretch.

They ate while he drove. There were plastic knives and small containers of butter and cream cheese—some of which were even flavored; Sheila went with a garlic one. Then regular cream cheese for the second bagel. Minka nibbled.

"Thank you for the bagels," Sheila said once she was stuffed. She felt bloated, but she welcomed it; she had not felt that way in quite a while.

"You're welcome," the man said, keeping his focus straight ahead. Both hands rested loosely on the top of the steering wheel.

"Who are you?"

The man peeked into the rearview mirror, made quick eye contact with Sheila, then looked back to the trail. "I can't tell you that."

"What about your name?"

"I can't tell you that, either."

Okay, interesting.

"Where'd the bagels come from?"

"Excuse me?"

"The bagels. Where'd you get them from?"

"What difference does it make?"

Fair.

She leaned back. The man seemed nice so she did not want to push her luck. As the truck bounced, the gentle vibration nearly put her to sleep. She fought to keep her eyes open for safety purposes, but it was quickly evident it was a battle she was likely to lose. She reached over for Minka and grabbed her hand. She squeezed. Her eyes got heavier.

Later, she startled awake in a cold sweat with a racing heart. Minka was there and awake, and she placed a hand on Sheila's knee, which almost immediately settled her. Sheila peeked out the window and was surprised at what she saw. Surprised and a bit worried.

Airplanes.

"Where are we?" she said, although the answer could not have been more obvious.

"Airport," the man said.

"Why?"

"I can't give you that information."

"Can't, or won't?"

The man looked back at her through the rearview mirror, but did not respond. It was all the same, anyway, was it not?

They parked and the man helped them out of the truck the same way he helped them in—graciously, by holding out a hand so they could use it for support as they stepped down. The truck's security system beeped and Sheila and Minka followed the man inside.

They were ushered to the front of every line, past angry or jealous onlookers, and bypassed security. Minka grabbed a hold of Sheila's hand and held on tight as they walked side by side, with Sheila a step or two ahead. They approached an unmarked gate and the man told them to hang out for a few seconds. Sheila sensed Minka was too overwhelmed to give them a chance to take off, but maybe that was just an excuse; running never seriously crossed Sheila's mind. Where would they run to? From whom would they have been running from? They did not even know who the man was, just that he was kind to them. Which, as she had learned, was not a trait every man possessed.

Sheila watched as the man presented a woman at the gate with a stack of papers. The woman took them, glanced at them, and pocketed them. Then she accepted a handshake from the man and turned to open the gate.

The man walked back toward Sheila and Minka. "This is where we depart," he said upon approach.

"Will you tell us why we're here now?" Sheila tried.

He ignored her.

She sighed.

"Good luck, ladies. I wish you well." The man nodded once and walked past them and disappeared into the crowd.

"Excuse me?" the woman at the gate nearly shouted to them. "This way, please."

Sheila squeezed Minka's hand tightly and started walking. She felt Minka's hesitation in the tug against her arm. The sisters were ushered down a long and narrow corridor by the gate attendant, around a corner, then another. At the end, another woman waited. The two women whispered to one another briefly—or, more accurately, the gate attendant whispered to the flight attendant while the flight attendant listened. After the quick conversation, the gate attendant smiled and walked past them, back toward where they came from.

"Right this way," the flight attendant said.

Sheila obediently followed, dragging Minka behind her.

"The rest of the plane will be boarding shortly," the flight attendant said as she escorted them to their seats. "Get comfortable. We're going to be in the air for a while."

"Remind me," Sheila said, trying a different tactic, "how long is the flight again?"

"We should touch down in Stockholm at this time tomorrow."

Stockholm. As in Stockholm, Sweden. As in a mere eight- or nine-hour bus ride to Lund.

As in back to where everything all began.

The flight attendant smiled. "Enjoy the flight."

# CHAPTER THIRTY-FIVE

*Present day.* Over coffee, Randolph had a heart to heart with his only son. He told Bruce everything—even the sensitive things; even the things he probably should not have. But it was time to come clean, to release the burden he had been carrying. It was time Bruce got the whole story so he might understand where Randolph was coming from and his motivations for doing everything he did. That was the only way Bruce might find it within himself to forgive Randolph and not shut him out of his life.

It was the final straw Randolph was grasping at, hoping for the best.

Much of what happened in Iowa and the road trip with Sheila across the Midwest that ensued, Bruce already knew. That had been discussed at length before, so Randolph skipped all that. He dove right in to where they left off—who he spoke to on the phone that night he was on Bruce's sofa; where he went after Bruce asked him to leave; whom he met with. He told Bruce about Gary and Benji and the bus station where Sheila showed up impersonating a cab driver. Then about the warning she gave him, and the psychological debate he had to grapple with—leave with her and get on Gary's bad side, or stay behind and risk being Gary's next victim.

He explained why Sheila tossed his phone into the river and why he had to get a new one with a new number—the number he texted Bruce on, just in case he needed to reach out for anything. He described what he remembered about California and the cruise ship, and how every day he questioned if what he was doing was the right thing. That lasted up until the final night, when Sheila told him everything—about her life growing up with her dad, how she was forced to run drugs for him in her backpack; how she felt abandoned once her sister was born; how much she adored that same sister; then about the chatter about sex trafficking, and about how she had to get out so she could save herself and her sister's life once she was older. Randolph noticed Bruce's expression soften when he told him about that, as if her story had struck an emotional nerve with him, just as it had Randolph. Which was why, through Sheila's tears and vulnerability that night on the cruise ship, he offered to help her save Minka. She did not ask; she never asked him for anything, he realized that night. The dad in him was sympathetic. He understood. More than she would ever know, since she was not a mother. Randolph saw it as his fatherly duty to help; if Minka's own father was not going to protect her, someone else had to.

When they arrived at the port in Hawaii, Randolph's decision was all but made; he was going with, wherever that journey took them. Turned out, that was Palau. Minka would meet them there if all went according to plan.

They were so close. Somewhere along the way, their path had been intercepted by Gary and Benji and most shockingly, Patricia—Bruce's mom, of all people. Somehow, that unfathomable trio of misfits showed up after Randolph and Sheila were captured. Bruce took that part hard; he had no idea she was even out. Neither had Randolph. He was still reeling about it too, in many ways.

Talking about what happened next was difficult. Emotional. Randolph cried; sobbed, really. Bruce briefly left the table at one point and returned with a small box of tissues with the lotion inside them. For Randolph, he said, although Randolph noticed his son's cheeks were a bit flushed too. It was hard for both of them. Not only to talk about it and express his love for this woman who was not his son's mother, but also to cry in front of him. Randolph was not sure it had ever happened. When Bruce was a boy, Randolph worked a lot. He saw him at nights and on weekends, but it was Patricia who did most of the parenting. It was she who wiped the runny noses and sat next to his bed with a bucket when his belly acted funny. He and Bruce grew closer as Bruce aged, but they were never that close. Which meant being vulnerable with his son, in what might have been his lowest point as a man, was not something that came naturally to him.

But if he was being honest, it felt so damn good.

They hugged it out for a long minute afterward. Despite the tears, Randolph felt better, as if a weight had been lifted. He and Bruce shared a real moment. One worth cherishing, even under the circumstances.

Randolph only faintly heard a phone ring before it stopped. Janet and Maxwell were in the other room, playing on the floor or watching a show or doing whatever it was they did together; Randolph would find out soon enough, because he had no plans to go anywhere ever again. This, Utah, was his home now.

Randolph excused himself and went into the bathroom. He struggled to drain his bladder as usual and noted to himself that he would finally call his doctor back in Iowa on Monday and get a referral for a local urologist; he had ignored his prostate problem for too long and it was not improving. The time had come to finally do something about it, even if that led to doing something he did not want to have to do. He washed his hands and splashed some water on his face, felt it soothe his pores under his scruff. He felt better already. The only way to move on was to move forward, not backward.

That was before.

Now was after.

Here it ends.

Back in the kitchen, Randolph immediately knew something was off. The energy had shifted. Neither Janet nor Bruce looked at him when he entered. Janet stood awkwardly next to Bruce, who held a phone against his ear but did not say much. Then, as if Randolph had just now walked into the room, Bruce looked up.

"Actually, he is," Bruce said into the phone. "Let me think about it, okay?" Bruce pulled the phone away from his face and covered the mouthpiece with his hand. He said to Randolph, "There's someone on the phone for you."

Randolph was completely taken aback. He nearly gasped. "For me?"

Bruce extended his arm and the phone hovered in the air between them. Randolph stepped forward and took it. After, Bruce rested a hand on Janet's back and led her out of the kitchen, leaving Randolph alone with the phone and the mystery caller on the other end. He felt his pulse quicken.

He put the phone to his ear and listened. Soft breathing. Footsteps. An inaudible voice or two in the background. He cleared his throat and said, "Hello?"

"Hi, Randolph."

He nearly fell over.

Some voices are impossible to forget—whether they elicit positive or negative memories, or just rock you to your core for one reason or another. Sometimes you just react without thinking. Especially when you were married to that voice for thirty-two years.

"Patricia?"

He realized, hearing her voice, that he had not dreamed about her in some time. Not since he visited her at the Iowa

Correctional Institution for Women. After seeing here there and all but freaking out, he thought he had not been ready to see her again. But then he saw her in Palau and did not lose control of himself, and so now he thought maybe it was all part of the healing process. Maybe by putting himself in that uncomfortable position then, it helped him to move on now.

Which did not mean that excluded him from being surprised to hear from her.

"Why are you calling me?" he asked her after she did not respond.

"Technically, I'm not. I called Janet. But if I'm being honest—which is a new thing I'm trying, by the way—I already tried calling you, but your phone isn't working."

Right. The river.

"Janet is a doll, isn't she?" Patricia said. "She's just the sweetest person. Bruce is so lucky to have her."

"Yes, I agree."

"I hope I don't get her in trouble. I know Bruce wouldn't talk to me, so I called her instead. I can't believe Max is going to have a baby brother in a few weeks!"

"A brother?"

"Yeah, she just told me. You didn't know?"

"Well, no. I guess I never asked."

"You've got to ask questions, Randolph."

Silence fell.

"I'm sorry," she said. "I don't get to do that anymore."

"Did you want something, Patricia?"

"What do you mean?"

"Why are we talking? What do you want?"

She sighed. "I just wanted to apologize."

"You've already done that."

"I know. But I am. Not just for Iowa, but for everything. I'm sorry for Gary. He was an asshole. I'm sorry for Palau. Our marriage. Your parents. I'm sorry for everything, really."

"What about my parents?"

Memories of the day he received a call saying his parents had died in a house fire rushed through him. The cause was later determined to have been a gas leak, though he never found out how it happened. Undetermined. They died peacefully in their sleep, thankfully. It was so long ago that he hardly ever thought about it anymore; just on or around the anniversary each year. Time healed all wounds, so it seemed. Which was an encouraging thought right now.

"I just don't think I ever told you I was sorry," Patricia said. "I should have been more supportive, and I'm sorry for that. I wasn't a very good wife."

"Why are you saying this to me now?"

"Just been reflecting. I've made so many mistakes."

"Not with Bruce."

"I'm sorry?"

"Not with Bruce. You were a good mom to him. He's an amazing man, and that's because of you. You should be proud of yourself for that."

He heard her sniffle.

"Thank you," she eventually said through the sniffles. "That means the world to me."

"I'll remind him of that. I'll send you photos of the baby if he doesn't. But I have a feeling he will. Where are you?"

"Back in Iowa. Same place."

"What happened to you in Palau?"

Patricia sighed again. "Long story. The short version is, some men showed up and bound my hands, and took me away. The asshole too. I had to sit in the back of a car with him the entire time. He's lucky I didn't spit in his face. I ought to have. Anyway, United States federal agents met us at the airport and sat next to me on the way back home. My hands were bound the whole time like I was some sort of criminal. Can you believe that? One of the idiots even had to feed me pretzels and hold the water up to my lips so I could drink. Completely degrading. Would it really have killed them to untie me on the airplane? Seriously. Not like I could go anywhere."

Randolph said nothing because he had nothing to say. Patricia, it seemed, still had a way to go in her journey, despite the best of intentions.

"Anyway, I don't know what they did with the asshole. All I know is that he was on a different plane. And frankly, I don't care what they did with him. He's a real asshole."

"Yes, I'm aware."

"But I'm back in Iowa now, like I said. And that's it. This is where I'll be for a while. You know, in case you need anything, which I'm sure you won't."

"Okay then."

"Okay. Well, I guess that's it. That's all I've got to say. Goodbye, Rand—"

"Patricia, wait."

"What?"

"I've been thinking too."

"Okay."

"And I forgive you."

She was silent.

"I'm glad your plan failed"—he tried to laugh, but it came out flat—"and I've learned a lot about myself in the process. It's a two-way street. I played a part in all this too. It is what it is at this point. Now everyone can move on with their lives."

"Thank you for saying that," Patricia said through more sniffles.

"Goodbye, Patricia."

"Bye."

Click.

Randolph looked up and saw Bruce and Janet standing in the doorway, both smiling.

"How much of that did you hear?" Randolph asked.

"Enough," Janet said with one of her booming smiles. Her hands slowly massaged her belly.

"Dad, there's someone here to see you."

"What? For me?"

Bruce nodded.

"Who could possibly—"

Bruce stepped aside. The guest appeared. It was not who Randolph expected, or hoped, it would be.

"Are you kidding me?" he said.

# CHAPTER THIRTY-SIX

*Present day.* Standing in Randolph's son's kitchen, Benji could not help but get a kick out of the expression on Randolph's face. Shock. Bewilderment. Maybe even disgust.

"I tried to call," Benji said. "But there's something wrong with your phone."

"So I've heard."

Benji was a free man, indeed. The dorky attorney had explained the terms of the agreement in detail, showed him all the lines in the document that said as much. In exchange for the information about Gary, Benji's slate was wiped clean. No record. They even expunged the eviction. It was a fresh break. He could start a new life.

After he signed the necessary documents at the airport and shook hands with Agent Weasley, Agent Jax, and the attorney—whose name he still did not know, nor did he care to know—he was asked where he wanted to go; the United States would fly him anywhere in the country at their cost. Just this once. Before he made his decision, he stepped away and listened to the voicemail that had slipped into his inbox while being interrogated. He trembled after he listened to it all the way through, once then twice, then thrice. He could not believe it. It might have been the best news he had ever heard.

Utah was his decision. He had to talk to Randolph one last time.

"I figured you'd be here," Benji said to Randolph.

"I'm an easy guy to find, apparently."

"What do you mean?"

"Never mind. Why are you here?"

"I'm free, man." He told Randolph about the deal he made with the feds.

"That's great, but . . . why are you here of all places? I'm happy for you, but I don't think we should—"

"Oh, no, don't worry. I'm not staying."

He saw Randolph exhale.

"I came to say goodbye."

Randolph perked up now.

"Hey, did you know that Gary's been working with Sheila's dad? He was getting money from him to track down his daughter. The money wasn't coming from INTERPOL."

"How do you know that?"

"I've figured it out all, man. Between talking with the feds and thinking about everything that happened on the plane, I've put all the pieces together. Want to hear it?"

"Why not?"

This is what happened. Sheila ran away from home in Sweden at sixteen to avoid being trafficked sexually. Her dad Hector, also King Crips, wanted her back so she would not tell the authorities what she went through as a kid—therefore incriminating him. Through his connections, he knew someone who worked for INTERPOL or could get him in touch with someone who did. However that happened—Benji did not much care about the details of it—Gary O'Reilly was that guy. Gary had shown a propensity to be a loose cannon by stretching the law and abusing his power, so was an easy target. Gary could use the resources available to him through INTERPOL to work on finding Hector's daughter—behind the scenes, of course, quietly—and Hector would supply him the capital he needed.

Meanwhile, other members of the Crips—like the skinheads in Fiji and Palau—were after Sheila too. Benji did not know for certain, but he presumed the most likely reason was that if they got to her first, they could use her as leverage to extract cash from Hector for her return. A ransom, if you will. Another plausible scenario was that Hector had paid a lot of men or groups of men to find his daughter, and the one or ones who did would get a large reward. Either way, it explained why Gary was quick to pull the trigger and eliminate his competition.

When it came to actually capturing Sheila, Gary had multiple chances in the United States. What made the most sense to Benji was that Gary was playing both sides of the fence. Sheila did have a blue notice on her—Hector was being investigated for years so a case was being built against him, and his runaway daughter seemed like a ripe opportunity to get more information to help bring him down—so if he captured her legally while still accepting cash from Hector, he could win twice—professionally, for one, and with some extra cash on the side from Hector. He could have had Sheila deported back to Sweden, cashed in from Hector, and if he was really slimy—which was likely—he could have handed information about Hector over too. And by bringing down someone of Hector's stature, it did not seem far-fetched to think that a promotion might have been in the cards for him.

And considering what they knew about him now, that was a scary thought. Give Gary even more power, and who knew how bad things might have gotten.

Maybe Gary was too cute. He should have grabbed her when he had the chance. Instead, he stumbled upon the attempted murder plot and latched onto it, using his credentials to make threats and promises he, in retrospect, may not have had the authority to make. But who were Benji or Randolph or Patricia, even, to know that? They all felt they had no other choice but to help him look for Sheila.

Gary's biggest downfall was his greed. In Fiji, he planted a bug in Benji's ear that Randolph was up to something shady, even though Benji always knew that was not possible. Now, he realized that was all to distract him. If Benji was focused on watching Randolph, Gary could make sure he covered himself in whatever he was up to. When Sheila and Randolph were on the way to Palau, Gary could have easily had them detained. But he did not. Why? The answer was simple now, the more Benji considered it. He must have learned that Minka had ran away too, and considering all the information he had on Sheila, he must have known Sheila's intentions. Which meant if Gary waited it out as long as he could, Sheila might lead him right to Minka too. Then Gary would be in for a double payday if he had both of Hector's daughters.

The worst part, Benji surmised, was what Gary's final intentions were in Palau. Benji had no doubt in his mind that if Minka had not snuck up on Gary and kicked his ass the way she had, Gary would have taken Sheila and Minka and put a bullet through Benji, Randolph, and Patricia's heads. They would all be dead and their bodies maybe never found. Gary might have given Hector his daughters back, or maybe he would not have. Predicting what Gary's next move might have been would have been impossible. And scary. It felt like every possibility would have been on the table.

Everything had to go right for Gary. There were so many loose ends that he could not have tied up. He would have slipped up somewhere and been exposed. Which he had, hence Agent Weasley and Agent Jax watching him. Gary had been in too deep and he lost. If he was not already, it was only a matter of time before Gary was locked in a federal prison for a very long time.

After Benji finished word vomiting, he took a breath and looked up. Randolph's son and daughter-in-law stood with agape mouths. Randolph simply smiled.

"You're a smart guy," Randolph said. "Anyone ever tell you that?"

"Well, actually, they offered me a job."

"Who?"

"The feds."

"Wow. I'm impressed. What are you going to be doing?"

"Nah, I didn't take it."

"No?"

"No way, man. That's not for me. Besides, I'm moving. Leaving the country."

"Where to?"

Benji pulled out his phone and opened his voicemail. "Listen to this." He pressed play and put it on speaker.

"Benji, it's me." It was the voicemail that came through when he was being interrogated. It was from Justice. "I didn't want to tell you this way, but I can't get a hold of you. You're not responding to my texts. I'm getting worried. You're going to be a dad, Benji. I'm pregnant. Call me, please! I need to know how you feel about this."

Message over.

Benji felt his smile grow from ear to ear.

"Benji, congratulations!" Randolph said.

"Thank you! I'm ecstatic."

"So you're going to Fiji, then?"

He nodded.

"I'm proud of you, kid. I really am."

Benji felt his heart warm.

"Promise me something, okay? One thing."

"What is it?"

"You have a fresh start. Take advantage of it. No more hacking. No more smoking. It's time step up and be a dad. Listen, I know I'm not your father, but—"

Benji stepped forward and wrapped his arms around Randolph's waist. It was true, Randolph was not his father. But he might as well have been. He was more a father to him in a short time than his own father ever would be.

They separated.

"I will," Benji said. "I promise."

"What about your family back home? Have you reached out to let them know?"

"No, that's not going to happen. You can't make someone want to be a part of your life. If they wanted to be, they would have already been. You taught me that."

"I did?"

"In your own way, sure. You just said it. I've got a second chance at life. I can be the dad for my kid the way my dad never was for me. I can't wait. I only hope I love my kid as much as you love yours."

Randolph turned and looked at his son, and they shared a moment of tenderness. Benji felt how much they loved each other, even through their differences. Not everyone had to agree all the time; that was okay. Love would take care of the rest.

Randolph turned back and said, "You're a good kid. Man now. You'll do great."

"You think so?"

"I really do."

They smiled at each other.

"Anyway," Benji said to the room, "sorry to barge in like this. I have to go now. My driver's waiting. I really just did come to say goodbye, and thank you."

"You have a driver?"

"I've learned a thing or two about negotiation. I'm a quick study." He smiled. "One flight turned into two, plus a driver, plus first class."

Randolph laughed.

"We were spoiled, what can I say? It was the one good thing Gary did."

With that, Randolph stepped forward and hugged Benji again, who hugged him back. After, Benji shook hands with Randolph's son, smiled at his daughter-in-law, and waved to his grandson on the way out the door.

He got into the back seat of the car and closed the door, realizing he did not get Randolph's new phone number, and also realizing that was on purpose. If he wanted to start over, he really had to start over. Leave the past in the past, move into the future.

That was before.

Now was after.

Here it ends.

The car left and off Benji went to start his new life, the same person but a new man.

*Justice, here I come.*

# CHAPTER THIRTY-SEVEN

*Present day.* Even twenty-four hours in the air was not enough time to prepare Sheila for what was to come. The eight- or nine-hour bus ride from Stockholm to Lund did not happen. Instead, a half-hour cab ride took them from the airport to Kronoberg remand prison across the city. The prison looked less a prison and more of an industrial building dropped into the middle of a busy city street.

She and Minka squeezed each other's hands as they were escorted through the prison. A gate opened and they were let into an open room with round tables and plastic chairs. They were told to sit and wait, which they did.

A few minutes after that, the gate opened again and in walked their dad, Hector, escorted by two uniformed men. Hector sat across from Sheila and Minka while the uniforms stayed near the gate. The rest of the room was empty.

"Did my guys treat you well?" he asked them.

Sheila had not seen her father in years. He had put on a lot of weight, especially in the neck. His hair had grayed on the sides. His eyes looked more sunken than the last time she saw him. He looked tired. She felt angry.

"Which guys would that be?" she said.

"The guys in Palau."

Her words were stolen.

"What, you didn't think I knew? Come on, sweetheart. You know me better than that."

"Don't call me that."

He held up his hands in surrender. "Of course, you're a grown woman now. I think we got started on the wrong foot. Can we start over? Let's start over."

Nothing.

"It's nice to see you," he said. "Both of you."

"I can't say I agree," Sheila said. She positioned her shoulders so that Minka was behind her just slightly.

He gave a sad, hurt smile. "You impress me, my daughter. You've grown into a beautiful woman."

Nothing again.

"Can I assume that's a yes? That my men treated you well?"

"We're here, aren't we?"

"So you are. That's good. My best men are faithful to me. I can't say that about all of them, I'm afraid. You're fortunate I was able to get my men out there."

"What are you saying?"

"I'm just saying that not everyone thinks the world of your dad."

"What, it's easy to make enemies in the drug world, is that what you're saying?"

"You're not wrong. Some men would rather take you all for themselves, or worse. Anything to stick it to the man who cut them off."

"Okay, Hector. Are we supposed to thank you?"

"Hector? You mean Dad?"

"No, I meant what I said."

"Fair enough. And no, you don't need to thank me. It's just how it is."

"Why are we here?"

"Can't a father want to see his girls without an ulterior motive?"

"You tell us."

"Well, there is one thing. But it's not for me."

Sheila crossed her arms. "I'm listening."

"Let's back up first, before we do that. Can we do that?"

Sheila waited.

"Good. I said it before, but it's worth repeating. I'm genuinely impressed by you, Sheila. You've been incredibly difficult to find. You deserve all the credit in the world for that. And the fact that I'm in here partially because of you, equally impressive. Listen, I know about the letters to Minka's school. At least now I do. I didn't then. Very clever, Sheila. Very clever. There was a long investigation into me because of that, among other things, did you know that?"

She did not, though she had hoped there would have been.

"I've been careful. I could have kept going, you know that right? I have methods of getting whatever it is I want. You should know that about me. You're sitting here right now, aren't you? Case in point. Something else you might not have realized about me is that I care about my family. Which is why I wanted to get caught."

Sheila looked at Minka, who was glazed over, staring through their father. In shock, maybe.

"I told them everything. Going back to when you were a kid. They offered me a deal that would reduce my jail time, but I didn't take it. I don't care about that. Not at this point in my life. I just wanted to see you. Both of you."

"You got caught on purpose so you could see us? How does that make any sense?"

"On the surface, it wouldn't. But your dad's a smart cookie himself, just like his daughters. I did make a deal, though. A deal for you."

"Excuse me?"

"Everything that happened when you were a girl, both of you, it was my fault. One hundred percent my responsibility. I told them that. You were both minors anyway. So in exchange for me, you two get to live your lives the way you choose. No strings attached. No nothing. You can stop running and start using your birth name again. You're off the hook."

Sheila tried to process it, but she could not. Not like this. What was she missing? "Why?"

"Like I said, I'm a family man at heart."

"If you're such a family man, why do what you did?"

Hector sighed and looked into space as if really pondering that question. It was the ultimate question after all. He looked back at Sheila and responded with: "Why? You won't like my answer, but here's the truth. I got caught up. Between the money and the power and the thrill of it all, I went overboard. I have no excuse for it, and I'm sorry. But my final gift to you is your life back. That's the least I could do. You're still both so young.

"So I told the authorities everything and you two, and your mother, are in the clear. And so I figured, what the hell, maybe the police can help track you down too. Between the tracking device in Minka's phone and the extra eyes, we were able to safely bring you both back in, before someone else tried to. My guys have been on her since she left home, hoping she'd lead us to you, and she did."

"You brought us all the way here to tell us that? Why not a phone call? Why not a letter?"

"If you weren't so difficult to find, maybe I would have. But I can't say for sure. I wanted to tell you face to face anyhow."

"So you've told us. Congratulations. Now what?"

"I also wanted to apologize. For everything I've done. More specifically, for Gary O'Reilly. It took me too long to realize that his intentions weren't pure. He was supposed to bring you in so I could talk to you, and that was it. I wanted to patch things up between us. I now realize he made your life more difficult than it needed to be, so I'm sorry. It wasn't supposed to happen like that. You don't have to worry about him anymore. He's in a penitentiary on the East Coast in the United States now.

"The truth is, back then, I wanted you back so I could talk you out of talking to the police about me. I was prepared to compensate you for your silence. But things have taken, shall we say, a turn for the worse in recent times."

"What are you saying?"

"Sheila, Minka, my daughters, the reduced jail time deal I was offered would do me no good. I'm not well. My heart is failing. I'm sure you think that's ironic, and I wouldn't blame you. Be that as it may, my heart is only operating at fifteen percent. It was eighteen six months ago. Sixteen two weeks ago. I'm fading fast. Your father's dying."

That explained the weight. He had not put on weight, necessarily, he was swelling from the fluid retention. A classic sign of heart failure.

"Once it gets to ten percent or lower, chances are I won't make it more than a day or two. That could be anytime now, really. Before you say anything, the answer is no. The doctors says there's nothing they can do. I've refused all treatment anyway. I've lived a full life and it's clearly my time, so why fight fate?"

The news took Sheila's breath away. Hector was her father. Was she angry with him? Yes. Did she like him? No. Did she want to talk to him? No. But did she love him? Maybe. As much as she did not get along with him or understand anything he ever did, that did not mean she wanted him dead.

"What about Mom?" she asked. The thought of her mother made Sheila feel sad.

"Ah, your mother," he said. "I'm glad you asked. That one tiny thing I want from you, from both of you, is about her. I want you to go see your mother—but not for me, do it for her. She's been through so much, and now she's alone. She misses you both so much. So please, go see her before she dies of loneliness."

Shelia had all the feels when the cab pulled up in front of their mother's house. The street still looked the same as it had when Sheila left, except many of the houses in the neighborhood had cracking paint or growing moss snaking from the chimney or just general signs of wear and aging. It seemed that while the world moved on, the neighborhood had gotten old and dull. And sad.

Sheila and Minka did not speak much on the long ride to their mother's house. Both thinking about their father, presumably, and what his imminent passing meant to them. For Sheila, it was sad but only moderately. Mostly, she felt sad for her mother who would be alone, and for Minka who was just a kid and trying to figure it all out inside her head. Tough thing to ask a kid to do, even if their father was not a good person. Really, Sheila would need time to process everything and analyze her feelings later. Now was not the time to worry herself with it; Hector did not deserve her thoughts.

"Are you ready?" Sheila asked Minka as they approached the step, the pull of the front door just above.

"I guess."

Sheila took her sister's hand in triumph and led her forward. It was Sheila who knocked.

A painstakingly long minute passed. Was their mother home? She must have been; where else would she be?

Finally the outdoor light flipped on, and Sheila heard the door's lock disengage. Minka squeezed hard.

It was the way her mother looked that struck Sheila first, not her expression. She looked old, almost elderly, with a wrinkled face and sagging skin and a hunched back that was not like that the last time Sheila saw her. She was not even that old. Her mother studied her as if unsure who she was, then did a double take after she looked at Minka.

"Oh, dear lord, my girls!"

Sheila broke down.

Their mother pulled them in and wrapped her arms around them both. Sheila remembered being six, then nine, then eleven and how much she missed her mother's affection. She felt like a child again in her mother's arms, and she did not fight it.

All three sobbed. Even after their mother coaxed them into the house and closed the door, they sobbed some more. It was the manifestation of fifteen years on the run coming to a head in the comfort of her mother's arms. In the comfort of the place that would always be home, even if it never would be again.

Sheila never wanted to leave her mother—the one person who was always there for her, until she was not—but she had to do what she had to do to survive. That was just how it had to be. Part of her sympathized with her mother because of the situation Hector put her in, but another part was unable understand how she let it happen. A mother bear was supposed to protect her cubs from predators, was she not? Even if that predator was pappa bear.

Their mother ushered them into the kitchen and hurried to put a pot of tea on. She pulled out chairs and wiped the table clean with a wet dish rag. She insisted on slicing up some cheese and pouring a sleeve of crackers on a plate between them, even if it was the last thing on Sheila's mind.

"Eat, eat!" their mother said.

Sheila tried to, though she did not have much of an appetite.

When the tea was ready, their mother poured them each a cup over rosemary tea bags and placed them on the table. Sheila did not have the heart to tell her mother she did not care for rosemary. Never had.

"It's so lovely to see you, sweetheart," Pihla, their mother, said. "Both of you."

Sheila found it awkward. Her mother spoke as if they were gone on a routine vacation and had not run away from home as teenagers. The tone failed to match the reality of the situation.

"I've missed you," Minka said.

"Me too, sweetheart. Me too." Pihla took a sip of her still steaming tea.

Suddenly, it felt like there was nothing to say. How was that possible?

"So, Mom, we saw Dad," Sheila said.

Pihla put her tea down. "You did?"

"We did. How long has he been like that?"

"Oh, dear, it feels like ages. It hasn't been that long, I realize, but it sure does feel that way. He was diagnosed with heart failure coming up on two years ago now."

"How are you doing with it?"

"Well, I've had a lot of time to process it, so I'm all right. Nobody wants to lose someone they care about, but that's part of living, I suppose."

Okay, true.

"How are you managing here by yourself?"

"It gets quiet at night, but I've got my garden to keep me busy. Me and Johanna across the street go on a walk nearly every day. Remember her, Minka? She has a daughter about your age. I'm thinking about getting a small dog to keep me busy. Maybe a bichon frisè."

Sheila took a sip of her tea. She noticed her mother eyeing it, and she figured she would ask sooner rather than later why she had not touched it. "I've been gone a long time, Mom. A really long time."

"I know that."

"I was sixteen. And Minka's only thirteen."

"I'm your mother, don't you think I know that?"

"Do you? You seem awfully cavalier about it."

"Sweetheart, I may not show it outwardly, but I've thought about you every single day since you left. And same for Minka. Just yesterday, I changed the sheets on both of your beds and remade them, just in case. I even fluffed the pillows. Don't ask me why. I just feel terrible about what you went through. I understand why you left."

"Why didn't you stop it?"

Pihla laughed. "Stop it? Do you know how many policemen tried to stop your father and couldn't? Your father was one of the most powerful men in Sweden. Do you realize that? You can't fight power with nothing."

"So you just let it happen?"

"It's not like I wanted to. What choice did I have?"

"I heard you talking one night. He asked you what you thought."

"And? You don't know your father, sweetheart. Not like I do. He may have asked the question, but we both knew the answer already."

Sheila considered that. She wanted so badly to believe her mother that it hurt.

"Sweetheart, if there was anything I could have done, I would have. You must believe that. I did what I could to manage. I got a call from school one day about an email that came from me, but it was an account they didn't recognize. I'm not stupid, okay? I knew it must have been you. Who else would it have been? So I said that yes, it was from me, made up a story about switching email providers on the fly.

"I can't tell you how many times over the years, even before you left, where the police would come over when your father was gone and you were at school and ask me to agree to plant recording devices and ask him specific probing questions. They could protect me, they said, but I knew better. I knew if your father found out, he might actually kill me. Not because he'd want to, but because he'd have no choice. A lot of people relied on him. And you needed me, Sheila, so I couldn't risk that. So I had to play this role of the happy, submissive wife, even though I was dying inside every day.

"Did I love your father? Yes, I did, of course. I do. And he loves me. I didn't approve of the things he did, even if all those things also allowed us to live a comfortable life. There are so many people out there who deal with worse. All you can do is live the life you were given and ask for forgiveness of your sins when the time comes. When it comes down to it, there's not much more a mother can ask for."

"How about not having her kids make drug deals for their father?"

"I understand your frustration, I really do. It eats at me every day still, but it is what it is. I'm just as happy as you are that you got out before anything really unfortunate happened."

"Did you even look for us?"

"No."

The bluntness took Sheila's breath away. "No?"

"No, because if I looked, that meant you might be found. And I didn't want you found. I wanted you to stay hidden and live your life. I wished I was a part of it, but that wouldn't be possible with your father around. So I had no choice but to let it go, let you go, and try to be happy with the life I had."

"But we're your kids."

"Always. I love you both more than you'll ever know. If you have children of your own one day, maybe then you'll understand. You see, even with your father gone, there are still men who stop by the house periodically. They don't always come in, but I see them on the street, just loitering. Your father's men will always be watching, for as long as I live. That's part of the deal. Lifetime protection."

"Protection?"

"Of course. The men come and make sure I'm safe, that no one tries to bother me. There are rivals, you know."

Sheila guessed that made sense.

"Come with us then," Minka said.

"Go where?" Pihla asked.

"To the United States."

"I can't do that."

"Why not?"

"It's these men, Minka. They'll follow me. And if they follow me, that means they'll be around you too. That's what they've sworn to do."

"By whom?" Sheila asked.

"Your father, of course. He wanted to make sure I'd always be protected."

"Is this really protection?"

"I'm alive, aren't I? I'm here and alive and healthy. The house is paid off. I never have to leave. I can go to sleep at night without the fear of never waking up again, even if there's only grayness on the other side. You don't want this life, trust me. You two need to be somewhere far away from me, somewhere far away from this. Somewhere you can live life in full color and enjoy it."

Sadness swept over Sheila. "Is this how you want to live the rest of your life?"

"Absolutely not."

"Then come with us."

"You're not getting it, sweetheart. These men will be with me wherever I go. Which could mean other people could follow too."

"Other people as in the rivals?"

"That's right. If I go with you, that means those bad men could try to do bad things to you since they'll know where you are."

Sheila understood it now. All of it. It clicked. Their mother did love them—more than anything. The most selfless thing she could do was let them go so they could live their own lives. Normal lives. Not like Pihla's life.

Sheila grabbed her mother's hand.

Pihla patted Sheila's fingers with her free hand, then pulled away and stood up. She left the room and returned a minute later.

"I've been saving these," Pihla said. She tossed one envelope on the table to Sheila, another to Minka. "I hoped you might come back one day. You don't have to open it right now. It's just a couple of numbers. Each of you has a bank account with enough money to last a lifetime, if you invest it wisely."

Sheila was so surprised that her hand shook and she could not even hold the letter. "I don't know what to say."

"You don't have to say anything. Sure, your father's job may not have been the most respectable profession out there, but it sure did bring in a lot of money."

"This is drug money?"

"That's one way to look at it. Another is that it's family money."

"Mom, I don't think—"

"Oh, hush, Sheila. You always were the stubborn one. Don't be silly about it. Take the money. There's no need to struggle. Life's hard enough as it is to have to worry about finances. Consider it the final gift your father left you."

Sheila thought about it. She did not want to take it for every moral reason in her being, but her mother was right; it would have been stupid of her to not just because of that. Irresponsible. And considering what her future plans were, the money would certainly make things easier.

"I almost forgot," Pihla said, "one more thing." She stood and went to the cabinet under the sink. She grabbed something from the drawer and brought it back to the table, where she set it down.

"What's this?"

"It breaks my heart, but it's the right thing to do. It's the only thing."

Sheila grabbed it—a stack of papers—and read through them. Maybe it was a mother's intuition; it was the exact topic Sheila wanted to talk about next. "Are you sure about this?"

"There's no other way, is there?"

It was a hard point to argue. This made the conversation so much easier.

"What's going on?" Minka asked.

"Minka, sweetheart," Pihla said, "do you want to live in the United States with Sheila?"

"I thought—"

"You're only sixteen. You're still a minor."

"But what about—"

"This is the document that will allow you to do that," Pihla said. "I've already signed it. Once Sheila signs it, it's a done deal."

Minka looked confused.

"I want your sister to adopt you, Minka. I want Sheila to be your legal guardian. It's the only way you can live there legally."

Minka took a minute to think about it, even if she and Sheila had spoken about it at length many times over. Talking was one thing, but acting on it when the time came was another. Sheila understood. Minka looked around the kitchen as if taking it all in for one last time. Tears pooled in her eyes.

"I know it's a tough decision, sweetheart, but I think—"

"I'll do it," Minka said. "I want to do it."

Pihla looked at Sheila. "Sheila?"

"Yes, of course."

Pihla uncapped a pen and handed it to her.

Sheila signed on the line.

"That's it," Pihla said. "I'll have my attorney handle the rest." She looked at Minka. "You'll always be my daughter. I want you to know that."

Minka nodded and stood up. She walked around the table and gave her mother a hug. Tears fell from Sheila's eyes as she watched.

"There's just one promise I need you to make me," Pihla said when they separated.

"What is it?" Sheila asked through tears.

"You need to come visit as often as you can." Pihla grinned.

Sheila smiled. Minka laughed.

"Deal," Sheila said.

# CHAPTER THIRTY-EIGHT

*Present day.* Two weeks after Benji came and went, Randolph had received no unexpected phone calls or visitors. No emails, no text messages. He was beginning to settle in to his new life, and it felt good. Janet was another week closer to becoming a mother for the second time. The name she and Bruce had picked out was Jadyn. Maxwell and Jadyn. A happy family.

Randolph had begun to put his life back together. He received a referral for a local urologist and saw him over a week ago. The PSA results came back with good news for once: No change. Which meant his prostate had not swelled any further. There remained no course of action since he had not worsened. Routine check-ups and daily monitoring was the prescription. Nothing he could not handle. The situation felt settled.

Patricia, Benji, and Gary were in the rearview. Gary was out of his mind completely. He felt confident that Gary would no longer be an issue in his life. With Benji, he also felt confident that he would turn his life around and mature into a good, decent father. There would be lots of challenges as he worked through that process, first with not knowing Justice hardly at all, then with trying to raise a baby while still growing up himself. But that was life; he was dealt a hand, and now he had to handle it. He would. When it came to Patricia, he finally felt a sense of closure. There were some things he would never understand about her or the decisions she made, and he was okay with that. She would work on rehabilitating herself while serving her time. It was up to Bruce whether he wanted her in his life, though Randolph would keep his word and at least send her a photo or two of baby Jadyn.

Bruce connected Randolph with a local realtor, who had begun showing Randolph around town a bit during the days. There were plenty of options, he learned, and budget was not much of a factor. He was deciding between two right now and would submit an offer either tomorrow or the next day. It just so happened to be a buyer's market, so he had the leverage.

What remained was the situation with Sheila. He had reached out many times without response. He was fearful for the worst but optimistic that she was handling things and would be in touch as soon as she could. As much as he tried not to think about all the scenarios and could avoid the negative possibilities while he kept busy during the day, at night was much more difficult. He would lay there awake, staring at the darkness of the ceiling, alone with just his thoughts. His mind would routinely wander to some dark, depressing places.

One Sunday during dinner, two weeks and two days after Randolph arrived, if he counted the night he collapsed on the porch, there was a knock on Bruce's front door. Usually a knock was just a knock—a nothing, mundane, everyday occurrence that happened at homes all across the world—but it was never just a knock these days. Everyone sprang up—Randolph, Bruce, and Janet—except for Maxwell, who was elbow deep in spaghetti sauce.

"You expecting someone?" Bruce asked Janet, who said she was not.

"Should I get it?" Randolph asked.

"If you want," Bruce said.

Randolph excused himself and wiped his face with his napkin, then went to answer the door. He turned the handle and pulled to door open and froze.

*Sheila.*

*Sheila!*

"Sheila!" he exclaimed. "What are you doing here?"

"Sorry for just coming over unannounced. I thought a surprise might be nice, but then I wondered if that was a bad idea. Was it a bad idea? Are you in the middle of something? I can leave and—"

"No, Sheila, definitely not. You're not going anywhere. I'm so happy to see you." His heart fluttered as he smiled at her. "Come here."

She walked into an embrace, followed by a long, wet, passionate kiss.

Randolph was so happy he thought he might float away.

After they separated, he noticed Minka for the first time, standing there on the porch with a roller bag behind her.

"Minka, hi," he said.

"Hi."

"Sorry," Sheila said. "I should have called."

"No, it's okay. What's going on?"

"She's with me now."

"Permanently?"

"Permanently." Sheila searched his face, waited for a response.

He did not have to think about it for a second. This had been her—and eventually his—end goal all along. "That's fantastic!"

Sheila smiled and sighed with relief. "Thank you. A lot's gone on. We have a lot to catch up on."

"How long do we have?"

Sheila shrugged.

"Staying?"

She nodded and smiled.

Randolph smiled back. Great news. "Come on in. I can make up a couple plates." He led them into the kitchen, where the others were. "Bruce, Janet."

They looked up.

"Sheila!" Janet said. She scooted her chair back and waddled toward Sheila, then pulled her into a hug. "How are you?"

"Happy to see you," she said. "When are you due?"

"Any day now!"

Bruce stood up now too and came over. "Who's this?" he said, meaning Minka.

"This is Minka," Randolph said. "Sheila's sister."

"Actually," Sheila said, pulling Minka in close, "she's more like my daughter."

Randolph was befuddled.

"I've officially adopted her. That way, she can stay with me permanently and I can get her a green card."

Everyone waited for someone else to be the first to respond.

It was Bruce. "Well, that's amazing. I'm happy for you. Are you hungry?"

Randolph had never felt prouder in his life.

"Pull up a seat," Bruce said. "We've got plenty of pasta. Janet can't seem to figure out the right amount to make."

"Hey!" Janet joked through a laugh. "If anyone has a trick, I'm all ears!"

"Thank you," Sheila said through a smile as she sat. "We won't stay long. Is there a good hotel nearby where we can crash?"

"Oh, sure," Janet said. "We'll figure that out later. Now, eat, before it gets cold!"

So that was what they did. They ate.

Until it was time to be done.

Janet grunted. The sound of trickling water rang through the kitchen.

"What's that sound?" Bruce asked. "Do you hear that?"

Someone gasped, maybe Sheila.

"I hate to spoil everyone's dinner," Janet said, oddly calmly. "But either I just peed, or my water just broke."

"Baby!" Randolph said, bursting from his seat. "We're having a baby! You got the checklist, Bruce? Who's got the checklist? Baby bag. Diapers. A change of clothes for mom and the baby. What else?"

Bruce laughed. "Dad, it's fine. The bag's all set. It's just in the other room."

Chairs scuffed the floor as Janet and Bruce and Sheila all stood up.

"Done!" Maxwell announced.

"Good boy," Randolph said. He scooped the crumbs from Maxwell's tray into his hand and tossed them on his own plate. "Here, let me clean up your face." Randolph wiped Maxwell's cheeks with a napkin. "Now, who's ready?"

"Dad, slow down," Bruce said.

Randolph scooped up Maxwell and tucked him under his arm. He made an airplane sound with his lips and shouted, "To the car we go!"

All he heard was laughter—first from Maxwell as he tried to spread his limbs and fly through the air, then from the crowd left behind in the kitchen as he nearly ran through the house, toward the front door, and out onto the porch.

The sound of family.

The family that would be getting a little bigger real soon. And Randolph would not have it any other way.

Here it ends.

Or maybe this was where his new life began.

# THE END

# AUTHOR'S NOTE

Dear Reader,

Thank you for joining Randolph, Benji, and Sheila on their journeys. That concludes the series, and their stories.

I would love to hear your thoughts on the book or the series as a whole. If you would consider sharing a few sentences about your experience with it anywhere you love to talk about books, I would be grateful.

Feel free to reach out via @danlawtonauthor on Instagram or Twitter, on Facebook at www.facebook.com/danlawtonfiction, or via email at info@danlawtonfiction.com. Also visit my website for updates: www.danlawtonfiction.com.

All the best,

Dan Lawton

# MORE TITLES BY THIS AUTHOR

*Now Was After (That Was Before #2)*

*That Was Before (That Was Before #1)*

*The Green House*

*Plum Springs*

*Amber Alert*

*Operation Salazar*

*Deception*

## ABOUT THE AUTHOR

Dan Lawton is an award-winning suspense and thriller author from New Hampshire. He is an active member of the International Thriller Writers (ITW) Organization. Awards include:

*The Green House*
- Bronze Medalist, Adult Fiction - 2020 Independent Publisher (IPPY) Book Awards
- Finalist - 2021 Montaigne Medal (Eric Hoffer Awards) for most thought-provoking book
- Finalist, Fiction - 2020 Next Generation Indie Book Awards
- Finalist, Mystery - 2020 Book Excellence Awards
- Finalist, Literary Fiction - 2020 American Book Awards

*Plum Springs*
- Winner, Fiction - 2019 New Hampshire Writers' Project Readers' Choice Award

Connect at @danlawtonauthor and danlawtonfiction.com.

# NOTE FROM THE PUBLISHER

Word-of-mouth is crucial for any author to succeed. If you enjoyed *Here It Ends*, please leave a review online—anywhere you are able. Even if it's just a sentence or two. It would make all the difference and would be very much appreciated.

Thanks!

We hope you enjoyed reading this title from:

www.blackrosewriting.com

Subscribe to our mailing list – *The Rosevine* – and receive **FREE** books, daily deals, and stay current with news about upcoming releases and our hottest authors.
Scan the QR code below to sign up.

Already a subscriber? Please accept a sincere thank you for being a fan of Black Rose Writing authors.

View other Black Rose Writing titles at
www.blackrosewriting.com/books and use promo code
**PRINT** to receive a **20% discount** when purchasing.